"O_____on,
Ba_____

_____ their
horses," Reeves said. "Bank robbers and killers who didn't
give me no choice."

"And why do I sense you're not happy about it?" Clint
asked.

"I ain't never happy about havin' to kill a man, Clint,"
Reeves said, "but this was different."

"Why?"

"Because they was black."

"There's more to it than that, isn't there?" Clint asked.

"Yeah, there's more," Reeves said. "They were former
Buffalo Soldiers—and I think the rest of the gang are also
former Buffalo Soldiers."

Clint knew that Reeves had gone to the Buffalo Soldier
Academy to learn how to be a proper lawman. Having other
men—even former Buffalo Soldiers—go rogue would not sit
well with him, at all.

"Are you determined to go after these men and bring
them back? Even though they were Buffalo Soldiers?"

"I am."

"Alone?"

"Well," Reeves said, "I need a favor."

Clint cut into his inch-thick steak and said, "Then I'm
your man."

DON'T MISS THESE
ALL-ACTION WESTERN SERIES
FROM THE BERKLEY PUBLISHING GROUP

THE GUNSMITH by J. R. Roberts

Clint Adams was a legend among lawmen, outlaws, and ladies. They called him . . . the Gunsmith.

LONGARM by Tabor Evans

The popular long-running series about Deputy U.S. Marshal Custis Long—his life, his loves, his fight for justice.

SLOCUM by Jake Logan

Today's longest-running action Western. John Slocum rides a deadly trail of hot blood and cold steel.

BUSHWHACKERS by B. J. Lanagan

An action-packed series by the creators of Longarm! The rousing adventures of the most brutal gang of cutthroats ever assembled—Quantrill's Raiders.

DIAMONDBACK by Guy Brewer

Dex Yancey is Diamondback, a Southern gentleman turned con man when his brother cheats him out of the family fortune. Ladies love him. Gamblers hate him. But nobody pulls one over on Dex . . .

WILDGUN by Jack Hanson

The blazing adventures of mountain man Will Barlow—from the creators of Longarm!

TEXAS TRACKER by Tom Calhoun

J.T. Law: the most relentless—and dangerous—manhunter in all Texas. Where sheriffs and posses fail, he's the best man to bring in the most vicious outlaws—for a price.

THE GUNSMITH

362

BUFFALO SOLDIERS

J. R. ROBERTS

JOVE BOOKS, NEW YORK

THE BERKLEY PUBLISHING GROUP
Published by the Penguin Group
Penguin Group (USA) Inc.
375 Hudson Street, New York, New York 10014, USA
Penguin Group (Canada), 90 Eglinton Avenue East, Suite 700, Toronto, Ontario M4P 2Y3, Canada
(a division of Pearson Penguin Canada Inc.)
Penguin Books Ltd., 80 Strand, London WC2R 0RL, England
Penguin Group Ireland, 25 St. Stephen's Green, Dublin 2, Ireland (a division of Penguin Books Ltd.)
Penguin Group (Australia), 250 Camberwell Road, Camberwell, Victoria 3124, Australia
(a division of Pearson Australia Group Pty. Ltd.)
Penguin Books India Pvt. Ltd., 11 Community Centre, Panchsheel Park, New Delhi—110 017, India
Penguin Group (NZ), 67 Apollo Drive, Rosedale, Auckland 0632, New Zealand
(a division of Pearson New Zealand Ltd.)
Penguin Books (South Africa) (Pty.) Ltd., 24 Sturdee Avenue, Rosebank, Johannesburg 2196,
South Africa

Penguin Books Ltd., Registered Offices: 80 Strand, London WC2R 0RL, England

This is a work of fiction. Names, characters, places, and incidents either are the product of the author's imagination or are used fictitiously, and any resemblance to actual persons, living or dead, business establishments, events, or locales is entirely coincidental

BUFFALO SOLDIERS

A Jove Book / published by arrangement with the author

PRINTING HISTORY
Jove edition / February 2012

Copyright © 2012 by Robert J. Randisi.
Cover illustration by Sergio Giovine.

ISBN: 978-0-515-15039-1

JOVE®
Jove Books are published by The Berkley Publishing Group,
a division of Penguin Group (USA) Inc.,
375 Hudson Street, New York, New York 10014.
JOVE® is a registered trademark of Penguin Group (USA) Inc.
The "J" design is a trademark of Penguin Group (USA) Inc.

PRINTED IN THE UNITED STATES OF AMERICA

10 9 8 7 6 5 4 3 2 1

ONE

Bass Reeves had been tracking the gang for weeks. Now he was closer than he'd ever been. The tracks ahead of him were as fresh as he had seen.

A former slave, the black man had been wearing a badge for many years, ever since he was freed. During those years he had learned his job by doing it. He certainly wasn't an expert tracker, but he had learned enough over the years to be confident that he was reading sign correctly.

The gang of eleven had split up, forcing Reeves to make a choice. He chose the trail left by two, figuring that when he caught them, they would tell him where the others were going.

As a black man wearing a badge, he was often the victim of double prejudice. Riding into the town of Muskogee, one of the towns that had been founded by the five tribes who inhabited this part of the region—the Cherokee, Chickasaw, Choctaw, Creek, and Seminole—he was regarded with suspicion for both reasons. But he sat his horse tall and ignored the stares.

The gang Judge Parker had sent Reeves after had robbed a number of banks in Arkansas, had killed several people in their most recent holdup. Parker wanted them back alive so he could hang them.

They had no descriptions of the men, as they wore masks in each of the banks they had robbed. Reeves had used word of mouth across the Territories to finally pick up their trail, and maybe today would be the day he'd catch a couple of them and find out who they all were.

He rode his horse to the livery and handed it to a wary white man.

"Keep him ready," Reeves said. "No tellin' when I'll need him."

"Yes, sir," the man said. He was impressed—or intimidated—by both Reeves's sheer size, and his badge.

"A couple of strangers rode into town ahead of me," Reeves said. "Did they leave their horses here?"

"No, sir, ain't nobody been here all day."

"What about yesterday?"

"No, sir."

"All right," he said. "You got a sheriff here?"

"Yessir, but he's an Injun."

"That don't matter to me," Reeves said.

"His name's Sam Overbay," the man said. "He's a Cherokee."

"Okay, thanks. I'll find him."

"You can't miss 'im," the man said. "He's probably the only man in town you'll have to look up to."

Bass Reeves drew himself up to his full six feet four and said, "That should make him easy enough to find."

He left the livery.

Bass Reeves found Sheriff Overbay sitting in a chair outside the sheriff's office, whittling on a block of wood with a huge knife.

"Sheriff?"

The Indian looked up at him, squinting against the sun.

"Saw you ride in," he said. "The sun was comin' off your badge. Deputy marshal?"

"That's right," Reeves said. "Judge Parker's court."

"What brings you here?"

"Tracked a couple of bank robbers here," Reeves said.

"Are you gonna kill them?"

"The Judge wants them alive," Reeves said. "That's my job. But in the end, it's gonna be up to them."

"Well," Overbay said, putting his block of wood aside and sheathing his knife, "a couple of strangers rode in earlier today."

"I asked the liveryman about that."

"They didn't go to the livery," Overbay said. "They went to the saloon."

Reeves turned, looked down the block, saw the word "Saloon" on one of the adobe buildings.

"Thanks."

"You want some help?"

"Don't think so," Reeves said.

"Well, if I hear shots, I'll come runnin'."

"That's fine."

Reeves turned to leave and the sheriff said, "It must be tough on you."

"Why do you say that?"

"Well, I don't like it when I have to throw my own people into jail," Overbay said. "I just thought you'd feel the same."

"My people?" Reeves looked confused.

"Oh, I thought you knew."

"Knew what?"

"The two fellas you're lookin' for," Overbay said. "They're black."

TWO

Reeves walked down the street with a bad feeling in the pit of his stomach. The only black men he knew of who were riding the Territories with guns were Buffalo Soldiers who were helping to uphold the law. He didn't like the idea of black men robbing banks and murdering innocent people.

He turned and looked behind him. Sheriff Overbay had picked up his block of wood and was once again worrying at it with his knife.

When Reeves reached the front of the saloon, he heard a few voices from inside, but it didn't sound like a busy place. He took a deep breath and entered through the batwing doors.

There was a short bar on the left with a couple of men standing at it. There was one bartender behind the bar, who eyed Reeves with distaste. In the back, sitting together at a table, were two black men, who perked up when they saw Reeves enter.

"Jesus," one of the men at the bar said, "another nigger."

"Where the hell are they comin' from?" his partner wondered.

"And why are they comin' to my place?" the barkeep added.

They hadn't seen the badge on Reeves's chest until he turned to face the bar. The bartender straightened up, reached beneath the bar.

"If you come out from under there with a shotgun, I'll have to kill you," Reeves said.

"You—You're Bass Reeves," one of the other men said.

"That's right."

Both men spread their arms so that their hands were away from their guns.

"We didn't mean nothin'," one of them said.

"You boys better get out, then," Reeves said. "I got other things on my mind, but if you stay here—"

"No, no," the other man said, "we'll go."

They made a wide circle around Reeves and left the saloon.

"You wanna cold beer, Marshal?" the bartender asked nervously.

"Don't mind if I do."

The bartender nervously put a beer in front of Reeves. He hoped none of his white customers would come in and see. He'd have to throw out the mug after the black lawman left. And also the glasses the other two black men were using.

"How long have those two been in here?" Reeves asked.

"Which two?"

"The only other two in here," Reeves said. "The two black men at the table. See 'em?"

"Oh, yeah, sure—"

"What's your name?"

"Eddie."

"How long have they been here, Eddie?"

"A couple of hours, I guess," the bartender said.

"Drinkin' the whole time?" Reeves asked. "Or nursing those drinks in front of them?"

"No, they pretty much been drinkin' the whole time."

"Drinkin' what?"

"Whiskey."

"That a fact?"

Reeves stared at the man, who averted his eyes and said, "Rotgut."

"Probably worse than that," Reeves said. "You wouldn't want to waste real whiskey on two niggers, would you?"

"Hey, I never said they was—"

"You got a shotgun under the bar?"

"Yessir."

"I want you to reach under there and unload it. Then put the shells on top of the bar."

"Yessir."

The bartender reached under the bar.

"You try and shoot me through the bar and I'll kill you. Understand?"

The bartender nodded nervously. Moments later he put two double-aught shells on the bar. If he had fired through the bar, he would have shredded Reeves, but he didn't have the nerve to try.

Reeves took the shells and put them in his pocket.

"Don't try reloadin'."

"No, sir."

Reeves finished his beer, slapped the empty mug down on the bar.

He turned and started walking toward the two black men.

"I'm tellin' you, man," one of the black men told the other, "dat man is Bass Reeves."

"Just relax," the second man said. "He might not be here for us."

"Why else would he be here?"

"Maybe jus' for a cold beer."

"I'm warnin' ya," the first man said. "If he comes towards us, I'm gonna cut him down."

"Yeah, okay," the second man said. "Jes' don't do nothin' stupid."

"Onliest thing that'd be stupid is to let ourselves get taken to jail," the first man said. "Dat Judge Parker would stretch our necks for sure."

"I'm jes' sayin' be careful," the second man said. "Let's jes' watch and see what—"

As he was speaking, Bass Reeves slapped his beer mug down and turned to walk toward them.

"Damn it—" the first man said, shoving his chair back and going for his gun.

"Aw, jeez—" the second man said, coming to his feet fast.

Reeves saw both men coming to their feet, both going for their guns. He wanted to yell for them to hold it and not be stupid, but he could see that he was way too late for that.

There'd be no talking.

THREE

As the two men went for their guns, Reeves reacted out of pure reflex. He drew and fired three times. Two bullets hit one man in the chest, one a perfect heart shot, the other one just insurance. Then he fired at the other men, and held himself back from pulling the trigger a second time.

The single bullet hit the man in the chest and his gun flew from his hand as he went down. Reeves rushed to him, hoping he could get a word or two out of him before he expired.

"Who are you?" he asked the bleeding man. "Who are you ridin' with?"

"Oh Lord, I's gonna die," the man cried. "Don' let me die, Mister Reeves!"

"I won't let you die," Bass Reeves lied. "Just tell me who you're ridin' with."

"Lord, save me!" the man shouted at the ceiling. "Don' let me die!"

Reeves shook the man and said, "I'll kill you myself if you don't tell me who you're with!"

"Soldiers!" the man cried.

"What?"

"B-Buffalo Soldiers," the man said, and died with a blood bubble on his lips. It popped and left dots of blood on his face.

Half an hour later Bass Reeves was sitting in the sheriff's office, looking across Overbay's desk at him.

"You're sayin'," the big Indian said, "that some Buffalo Soldiers are robbing banks and killin' people in the Territories?"

"Ex-Buffalo Soldiers," Reeves said. "I mean, I'm sure they're ex-Buffalo Soldiers."

"Were you once a Buffalo Soldier?" Overybay asked.

"No," Reeves said, "I enlisted in the Buffalo Soldier Police Academy, to learn how to be a proper marshal."

"From what I hear, you learned pretty good."

"I learned what I needed to in the Academy, but I learned the rest on the trail."

"Well," Sheriff Overbay asked, "what are you going to do now?"

"I have to go back to Fort Smith, with the two bodies," Reeves said. "Judge Parker needs to know what we're up against."

"Don't you mean," Overbay asked, "what you're up against? I'll bet Judge Parker ain't about to get on a horse."

"You're probably right about that," Reeves said, "but there is someone who will."

* * *

Clint Adams had been in Fort Smith for a week. After tracking a crooked sheriff from Adobe Walls, Texas, to the Territories and killing him, he decided to stay in town for a while. He wanted to rest not only his own bones, but those of his horse, the Darley Arabian, Eclipse.

While in Fort Smith, he had established contact with his friend, Deputy Marshal Bass Reeves. But after Bass Reeves was sent on a job by Judge Parker, Clint established contact with a new friend.

Her name was Rachel.

She had black hair, creamy white skin, and the most wonderful, full breasts he'd come across in some time. They were almost pear-shaped, with heavy, rounded undersides and large nipples and aureoles. Clint could have spent most of the afternoon on those breasts, but Rachel wasn't able to lie still that long.

She had plans of her own.

FOUR

Bass Reeves rode into Fort Smith with two bodies slung over their horses. It was not an unusual sight to the people of Fort Smith. Neither was it an unusual sight to Judge Parker, who happened to be looking out the window of his office at the time.

"Henry!"

The Judge's bailiff, a little man named Henry Butler, came rushing into the room—that is, as much as a slow-moving man like Butler could rush.

"Deputy Reeves just rode into town with two dead men. Did I or did I not instruct him to bring those men back alive?"

"You did, sir."

"Then why do you suppose he's got them slung over their horses like two sacks of sugar?"

"Uh, perhaps they didn't give him much choice in the matter, sir?"

"Well," Parker said, fiddling with his mustache, "I'll want to hear that from him, won't I?"

"Yes, sir."

"Bring him directly to my office as soon as he comes in."

"Yessir."

"And Butler!"

"Yes, sir?"

"Is Clint Adams still in town?"

"He is."

"And Heck Thomas?"

"He's out on an assignment, sir. Won't be back for . . . well, weeks."

"Well, if Marshal Thomas is out of town, why is Adams still here?"

"I believe he's made the acquaintance of a lady, sir," Butler said.

"A lady?"

"Yes, sir."

"Of dubious distinction?"

"I'm sure I don't know, sir," Butler said, "but word has it Mr. Adams does not dally with . . . whores."

"Is that a fact?" Parker asked. "A man of principle, huh?"

"Some principles, yes, sir," Butler said.

"All right," Parker said. "Get out. Bring me Reeves as soon as he arrives."

"Yessir."

Reeves delivered the two dead outlaws to the undertaker's, then took his horse to the livery stable behind Judge Parker's barracks building.

"Clint Adams still in town?" he asked.

"His horse is here," the liveryman said. "I don't think he'd go anyplace without him."

"Thanks."

Before he went home, before he got a steak or a beer, Deputy Marshal Bass Reeves went to the barracks building that housed not only the jail cells and courthouse in Fort Smith, but also Judge Parker's office. He presented himself to the little bailiff, Henry Butler, who regarded the big black deputy from behind a rather small desk that matched his own stature perfectly.

"The Judge saw you ride in," Butler said. "He wants to see you right away."

Reeves made a face.

"He ain't happy, huh? Well, them fellers didn't leave me much choice," he said.

"That is what I, ah, suggested to the Judge," Butler said. "You can go right in."

"Thanks, Butler."

Butler nodded as Reeves headed for the door to the Judge's office.

"Ah, Deputy Reeves," Parker said, spreading his arms expansively. "Welcome back. I see you brought back two of your prey—dead!"

"I can explain, sir."

"Good," Parker said, "then do so."

Parker was Eastern educated and, despite time spent in the West, maintained all those traits.

Reeves explained what had happened after he tracked the men to Muskogee.

"They gave me no choice, went for their guns right away," he said. "I have a witness, the bartender in the saloon—"

Parker waved Reeves off and said, "I don't need a witness, Deputy. If I can't believe my men, who can I believe? I accept you had no choice, but this was just two of the men."

"Yes, sir."

"There are more." It wasn't a question; it was a statement they both knew to be true. "Where are they? Did either of these men tell you that before they unfortunately died?"

"No, sir," Reeves said. "One of them spoke, but he only said two words."

"And what were they?"

Reeves hesitated.

"Well? Spit it out, man!"

"Buffalo Soldiers."

FIVE

Parker stared at Reeves.

"In what context did they say that?"

"I asked him who he was with."

"And he said, 'Buffalo Soldiers'?"

"Yes, sir."

"What did you think he meant by that, Deputy?" the Judge asked.

"That the bank robbers and murderers they were riding with were black men," Reeves said, "and ex-Buffalo Soldiers."

He could see that the thought of lawmen—even black Buffalo Soldiers—killing people made the Judge uneasy.

"That's not necessarily true."

"I hope you're right," Reeves said, "but I feel that you are not."

"Oh? Why?"

"There was no reason for the man to tell me a lie," Reeves said. "He was dyin'."

"So you're going back out?"

"Yes, sir."

"But if you're hunting Buffalo Soldiers—ex-Buffalo Soldiers—they will be . . . formidable."

"Yes, sir," Reeves said. "They should be well-trained men."

"I don't have another man to send with you," Parker said almost apologetically.

"I understand that, sir," Reeves said, "but I have an idea."

"What's that?"

"Can I tell you tomorrow mornin'?"

"Yes, all right, Deputy," Parker said, sounding weary now. "Get some food and a night's sleep. I'll see you in the morning."

"Yes, sir," Reeves said. "Thank you, sir."

Parker went to his window and watched as Bass Reeves left the building. He had no doubt what Reeves's idea was. He wished him luck.

Reeves left Parker's office and walked to one of Fort Smith's hotels. He went to the clerk and asked for Clint Adams's room number.

"Um, am I supposed to tell you that, Deputy?" the clerk asked.

"Yes, you are," Reeves said.

"B-But . . . Mr. Adams ain't alone," the clerk said. "And if I disturb him—"

"But you ain't gonna disturb him," Reeves said, "I am."

The clerk gave him the room number. He went up the stairs and down the hall, wishing he didn't have to interrupt his friend.

But he had no choice.

Clint rolled Rachel onto her back. Her solid breasts barely moved, but he knew that wouldn't last. When she was thirty or so, they'd start to sag, but right now—she was twenty-five or -six—they were perfect.

He lowered his mouth to her brown nipples, nibbled them, licked them, sucked on them while she held his head in her hands.

"You really like them, don't you?" she asked. "They're just tits."

"I like them, and you," he said, kissing her. "You—and they—are magnificent."

"Mmm," she said, pushing him off her and rolling him over. "Let me show you what I like."

She kissed her way down his body until she had his swollen cock in her hands. She lowered her lips to the head, stuck out her tongue, licked him lovingly. She wet the head thoroughly, then slid the length of him into her hot, eager mouth.

The sensation caused Clint to lift his hips to pump his cock in and out of her mouth. He knew from past experience—only hours past—that when he came, it would be as if his head were going to come off. She knew just how to suck him, how to milk him, how to stave off the end until he couldn't stand it anymore.

She sucked him lovingly, putting her hands beneath

him to cup his buttocks and pull him into her mouth even harder . . . and that's when the knock came at the door.

"Christ," Clint said. "Now?"

She lifted her head and looked up at him.

"Don't answer it."

The knocking came again, harder.

"Clint! Come on, man," a deep voiced rumbled. "It's Bass."

"Uh-oh," she said with a mischievous look on her pretty face, "it's the law."

"Don't go away," he told her, rolling off the bed and grabbing his gun.

He walked naked to the door, gun in his right hand just in case, and opened the door with his left.

"I'm impressed," Reeves said.

Clint looked down at himself. Although his cock was wilting, it was still mostly hard. But Clint didn't think there was much for Reeves to be impressed with—unless he was talking about the girl on the bed.

"Bass," he said, "I'm a little busy."

"That's what the clerk told me," Reeves said, "and I can see that, but I bet she won't go nowhere if you and me go out for a steak. My treat."

"Steak dinner?"

Reeves nodded.

"All the trimmings?"

"Whatever you want," Reeves said. "I need to talk to you."

"About what?"

"A favor."

"What kind of favor?"

"I'll tell you over a steak."

"Stay there," Clint said, and closed the door.

As the door closed in his face, Bass Reeves did see the girl on the bed—and he was impressed. His friend always had a way of finding women who were more than pretty—and they always liked him.

It was obviously a gift.

He walked back to the bed, holstered the gun, and picked up his pants.

"You're leaving?" she asked.

"The truth is, Rachel," he said, "I'm still worn out from earlier in the day. I need to fortify myself."

"And what about me?" she asked, rolling onto her back and staring at him. "I don't need to be fortified?"

"Get something to eat," he said, pulling on his boots and grabbing his shirt. "I'll meet you back here."

As he headed for the door, she said, "You hope."

SIX

O'Boyle's served the best steak in Fort Smith. It was a restaurant that Judge Parker usually frequented, but not as early as Reeves and Clint were there.

They both ordered steak dinners with everything, along with big icy mugs of beer. The waitress started them off with a basket of hot biscuits and butter.

"Okay," Clint said, buttering a biscuit, "what's going on, Bass?"

"I just rode in today with two dead men slung over their horses," Reeves said. "Bank robbers and killers who didn't give me no choice."

"And why do I sense you're not happy about it?" Clint asked.

"I ain't never happy about havin' to kill a man, Clint," Reeves said, "but this was different."

"Why?"

"Because they was black."

They sat back while the waitress set their steaming plates in front of them.

"There's more to it than that, isn't there?" Clint asked after she'd left.

"Yeah, there's more," Reeves said. "They were ex-Buffalo Soldiers."

"Jesus," Clint said. He could see why Reeves was so upset.

"There's more."

"More?"

"I think the rest of the gang are also ex-Buffalo Soldiers."

"How many?"

"I'm not sure," Reeves said. "Nine, maybe ten."

"Are you going after them?"

"Yes."

"Alone?"

"Well," Reeves said, "that's the favor."

"I thought it might be."

"The Judge has no one to send with me."

"Where's Heck?"

"Out on an assignment," Reeves said. "So are all the other deputies."

"Are you determined to go after these men and bring them back, Bass?" Clint said. "Even though they were Buffalo Soldiers?"

"I am."

Clint knew that Reeves had gone to the Buffalo Soldier Academy to learn how to be a proper lawman. Having other men—even ex-Buffalo Soldiers—go rogue would not sit well with him at all.

Clint cut into his inch-thick steak and said, "Then I'm your man."

After dinner they had pie. They didn't have Clint's favorite peach, so they both had apple pie, and hot, black coffee.

"What's your goal, here, Bass?"

"My goal?" The big black lawman frowned, unsure of what Clint meant.

"Usually you just want to bring the men you're hunting back here to deliver to the Judge. You don't much care what happens after that."

"That's true."

"I would bet this has got to be a lot different," Clint said.

"Yeah, it is," Reeves said. "I guess I wanna know what made them do what they're doin'. I mean . . . these men were Buffalo Soldiers. They used to keep the peace, and protect people." He shook his head. "Now they're out there killin' people."

"And you want to know why."

"Damn right I do."

"But you do still intend to bring them back, right?" Clint asked.

"I do."

"No matter what?"

The big black lawman frowned again.

"What are you gettin' at?"

"I'm willing to go along with you and watch your back, Bass," Clint said. "I just want to know exactly what we're doing, and why."

"We're huntin' lawbreakers, and we're gonna bring 'em back," Reeves said. "it's jus' . . . before we do, I wanna talk to 'em."

"Okay," Clint said. "When do we leave?"

"I gotta see the Judge in the mornin'," Reeves said. "I figure after that."

"Want me to meet you there?" Clint asked. "See the Judge with you?"

"Yeah, that'd be good."

Clint figured Judge Parker would want to see him anyway. Every so often the man offered him a deputy marshal's badge. Clint always turned him down, but that didn't phase the man. He kept trying.

"He's gonna try to make you wear a badge," Reeves said, as if reading Clint's mind.

"I know it," Clint said. "Don't worry. The Judge and I have an understanding."

"Okay," Reeves said.

"What are you going to do tonight?"

"Get some rest," Reeves said.

"Good idea," Clint said. "I'll do the same."

"Really?" Reeves gave Clint a look.

"Well," Clint said, thinking about Rachel, "I'll try."

They left the restaurant and Reeves walked Clint back to the hotel.

"I'm sorry you have to go through this, Bass," Clint said. "I know what the Buffalo Soldiers mean to you."

"It just ain't right," Reeves said. "It's hard for a black man to get respect, but that's what bein' a Buffalo Soldier means. These men . . . they're just pissin' on all of it."

Clint clapped his friend on the back and said, "Don't worry. We'll get them."

"Yeah," Reeves said, "you're damn right we will."

SEVEN

Clint did the best he could to rest that night, but Rachel was having none of it.

"If you're leaving tomorrow," she said when they got back to his room, "you're gonna make me happy tonight."

And he did, but she also did her part.

As he left the hotel early the next morning, he walked on shaky legs to the livery. He saddled Eclipse and rode him around to the barracks building where the Judge and his court were.

He waited in front for Bass Reeves to appear. The big black lawman came walking up leading his big steel dust behind him.

"Ready?" Reeves asked.

"I'm ready."

They went inside, presented themselves to Henry Butler first.

"Why doesn't this surprise me?" the bailiff asked. "Go on in."

Reeves and Clint entered the Judge's office.

"Well, Deputy Reeves," the Judge Parker said, "I'm assuming this was the idea you were talking about yesterday?"

"Yes, sir."

"Mr. Adams," Parker said, "for a man who refuses to wear a badge, you end up assisting my deputies very often. First, Deputy Thomas some time ago, and today, Deputy Reeves."

"They may be your deputies," Clint said, "but they're also my friends."

"So you're doing this as a favor?"

"Yes, sir."

"Which I assume means you still won't wear a badge,"

"That's what it means," Clint said, nodding, "yes, sir."

"Well," Judge Parker said, "at some point I guess I'm just going to have to get that fact firmly implanted in my head."

Clint didn't answer.

"When are you leaving, Deputy?" Parker asked, turning his attention to the man in the room who was wearing a badge.

"As soon as we're finished here, sir."

"Well," Parker said, sitting back in his chair, "as far as I'm concerned, we're finished."

"Yes, sir."

Reeves led the way to the door. As he opened it, Parker said, "Alive, Deputy."

Reeves turned.

"I want those men alive," Parker said, but then he relented somewhat and added, "If you can."

"Yes, sir."

Outside the barracks building they mounted their horses.

"What about supplies?" Clint asked.

"I've got some beef jerky and coffee," Reeves said. "And a pot."

"That should be enough," Clint said.

Reeves grinned.

"I learned to travel light from you."

"I don't think you need to learn much from me, Bass," Clint said.

"Then let's go."

"Where?" Clint asked.

Reeves waved his arm.

"Out there."

"Can we be more specific?"

"Well," Reeves said, "I found the men I killed in the northeastern part of the Territories."

"So you think that's where the others are?"

"No," Reeves said.

"Then where?"

"Let's ride," Reeves suggested, "and I'll tell you along the way."

Judge Parker walked to his window and looked down at Clint and Reeves, who were riding out. He spent a lot of time at this window. He usually watched his deputies ride out on their assignments, he surveyed the town quite often from there, and on days when there were hangings—very often four and five men at a time—he watched the proceedings from there.

In turn, seeing the Judge in his window from the street was a common sight. Parker felt this was a good way to let the people of Fort Smith know that he was on the job.

EIGHT

"So you think the two men you killed were . . . what? Waiting to meet the others?" Clint asked.

"I do."

"Why?"

"Because," Reeves explained, "that's what they were doin' when I found them—just sittin' and waitin—and drinkin'. Probably lucky for me they was drinkin', made them a little slower to react. I mean, quick to decide to go for their guns, but slow in actually drawin'."

"And you want to go back there?"

"Yes."

"If the others got there after you left, they've either moved on, or . . ."

"Or they're waitin' for me there," Reeves said. "They'll find out I killed two of them, and they'll want justice."

"Justice?" Clint asked. "Not revenge."

"They're Buffalo Soldiers."

"Ex-Buffalo Soldiers," Clint reminded him.

"Yeah, but they'll still think of it as justice."

"Okay," Clint said, "so if they're there when we arrive, we take them."

"Right."

"And if they're not there?"

Reeves shrugged.

"Then we do what we always do," he said. "We track 'em."

"That's what you always do, all right," Clint said, nodding.

"Hey, didn't you say you tracked somebody all the way from Texas to here?"

"I didn't have much of a choice," Clint said. "The man was a crooked lawman who shot a friend of mine. I wasn't about to let him get away."

"So then you understand," Reeves said, "and now you are here to keep me from gettin' shot by a bunch of crooked lawmen."

"Ex-lawmen . . . but I get it. How many days out is Muskogee?"

"It's almost ninety miles," Reeves said.

"That far?" Clint said. "Maybe we'll run into these ex-Buffalo Soldiers between here and there."

"I doubt it," Reeves said. "They will be ridin' away from Fort Smith, not toward it."

"Right."

"But we can be ready," Reeves added, "just in case you're right."

* * *

Sergeant Lemuel Washington surveyed his assembled men. The eight of them looked as if they hadn't had a wink of sleep among them.

"Corporal!" he shouted.

"Yessuh!" Corporal Adam Jefferson stepped up in front of Washington.

"Tell the men to saddle their horses and get mounted. We're movin' out."

"Yessuh," Jefferson said. "Uh, sir?"

"Yes, Corporal?"

Do we know what happened to the two men who were waitin' here for us?"

"Yes, we do, Corporal," the sergeant said. "They were killed by Deputy Bass Reeves."

"Sir . . . how?"

"According to a witness, they were foolish enough to go for their guns when Reeves entered the saloon. He killed 'em both."

"They were good men, sir."

"Obviously not good enough," Washington said. "Bass Reeves is a hard man, and he took them easy."

"Yessuh."

"Get them mounted, Corporal."

"Yessuh."

The men mounted up and then crowded around Sergeant Washington.

"We split up from here," he said.

"What?" One man spoke, but he spoke for all.

"There are nine of us," Washington said. "Two of you will go with Corporal Jefferson. Two of you will go with me. And two of you will go with Private Edwards."

"Go . . . where?" Edwards asked.

"I will tell you all where to go, what to do, and where to meet up with us," Washington said. "We have a dangerous man trackin' us, and we can't stay together, or do our next jobs together. We must make it hard for Bass Reeves to track us."

"Bass Reeves?" one of the soldiers said, his eyes popping.

"Yes," Washington said. "He killed Rafe and Lou."

The men exchanged glances and a buzz went through them.

"Then we should kill him," one of them said.

"And we will," Washington said. "Believe me, the time will come, but I'll say when. But right now I wanna talk to Jefferson and Edwards. I'll explain to them what we're gonna do, and they'll explain it to the rest of you."

He rode off, and Jefferson and Edwards followed him.

NINE

Sergeant Lemuel Washington knew his men well—all of them. He knew them well enough to predict what they would do in any situation.

He was talking directly to his corporal, Jefferson, but his words were really intended for Private Luke Edwards.

Although only a private in the Buffalo Soldiers, Edwards had the most experience of any of the men, and was a bit older than Corporal Jefferson, so when Washington needed someone to lead, he chose Luke.

Both men remained silent while their leader spoke, working on Luke's head. But Washington could tell, by the look in Jefferson's eyes, that the corporal knew what his boss was doing.

When they were done, they went back to the other men.

"Corporal, choose your two men."

Since Jefferson knew what Washington was planning, he knew which men to choose.

"Carl and Webster."

"All right," Washington said. "Gordon and Franklin, you're with me."

That left the two least experienced men, Bush and Davis, with Edwards.

This was the mix Washington wanted. Edwards had a lot of anger in him, and Bush and Davis were always ready to be led.

"Your leaders have your assignments," Washington said. "Go."

They rode out of town together, but soon after they split up.

After the others had ridden away, Washington turned to his two men, Gordon and Franklin.

"Do you think it's gonna work, Sarge?" Franklin asked.

"Is what gonna work?"

"Come on . . . sir," Gordon said. "You knew what would happen if you gave Edwards both Davis and Bush. Those boys'll do anythin' he tells 'em."

"Edwards is a leader," Washington said. "He'll lead them well."

"But you know what they'll do," Franklin said.

"Yeah," Washington said, "I know. Now, here's what we're gonna do . . ."

When they had cleared the others, Private Edwards held up his hand to halt their progress.

"What's wrong?" Bush asked.

"We're goin' the other way," Edwards said.

"Why?" Davis asked. "Is that what the sarge said we should do?"

"No," Edwards said. He stared at the two younger men. From appearances, he could have been forty or seventy. In truth, he was close to sixty, had spent many years in the saddle, even as a slave. He had a lot of bitterness in him, which was why he was following Sergeant Washington on these raids.

"I don't know about you, but I don't want that Bass Reeves on my tail," Edwards said, "so we're gonna go back and take care of him."

"The sergeant said he'd tell us when to do that," Bush said. He shifted nervously in his saddle.

"He did tell me," Edwards said.

"When?" Bush asked.

"When he pulled you and Jefferson away from the rest of us?" Davis asked.

"That's right."

"He told you to kill Bass Reeves."

"He didn't say it in them words," Edwards said, "but that's what he wants us to do, and that's what we're gonna do."

"How?" Davis asked. "We don't even know where the lawman is."

"We know two things," Edwards said. "He's gonna be trackin' us, and he's gonna go to Muskogee."

"How do we know that?" Bush asked.

"Experience," Edwards said.

"But—"

"You boys are gonna have ta stop askin' silly questions," Edwards said, "and just do what you're told. Ya got it?"

"Yes, sir," Bush said.

"Yeah," Davis said.

"Okay," Edwards said. "We're gonna turn around and go back, and then keep goin'. We'll run into Bass Reeves, and then we'll kill 'im."

"Are you—" Bush started, then remembered he wasn't supposed to ask any more questions.

"Ready?" Edwards asked.

The two men nodded. They were ready to follow Edwards. They just weren't sure they were doing the right thing.

TEN

Reeves figured that his horse and Clint's could cover the ninety miles in two days. They camped on the trail the first night, made a fire, and put on a pot of coffee. Then Reeves passed over some beef jerky.

"Sorry there's no beans," Reeves said.

"That's okay," Clint said. "I'm used to traveling light and keeping a cold camp. At least this way we have hot coffee."

"And strong," Reeves said, pouring it out. "I remember you like your trail coffee rough."

Clint sipped and found that Reeves was right on the money. This was rough coffee. And good.

"Should we set watches?" Clint asked.

"I think so," Reeves said. "I expect them to be runnin', but that don't mean they won't decide to double back on us."

"I'll take the first watch, then," Clint said. "Keep the fire going, and the coffee."

"Suits me," Reeves said, "but I ain't ready to turn in yet."

They sat together awhile, catching up and drinking coffee. Clint made another pot and they drank that before Reeves was finally ready to bed down.

"I'll wake you in four hours," Clint said.

"Jus' don't fall asleep yourself," Reeves said.

"I'll try not to."

In the morning Reeves woke Clint using the tip of his boot and handed him a cup of coffee.

"I already stomped out the fire," the black man said. "Drink that and we'll be on our way."

"Think we'll make Muskogee today?" Clint asked.

"We'll make it."

They broke camp and saddled their horses, mounted up, and started riding.

"It feels like I just did this," Clint said.

"What?"

"Rode to hell and gone tracking some outlaw," Clint explained. "I guess I should've left Fort Smith when I had the chance."

"Yeah, but you couldn't leave without seein' your friend Bass, could ya?" Reeves asked with a wide, white grin.

"No, damn it," Clint said, "I couldn't."

"So it's your own damn fault," Reeves said. "Stop bellyachin' about it."

"Stay here," Edwards told the other two, handing Bush his horse's reins.

He moved ahead on foot, then got down on his belly. His eyes were as good on that day as they had been when he was a kid. He could see two riders in the distance, could tell one of them was a big black man wearing a badge, while the other was white.

He crawled backward, then got to his feet and ran to Bush and Davis.

"He's comin'," he said, remounting his horse, "and he's got somebody with him."

"Another lawman?" Bush asked.

"Don't look like it," Edwards said, shaking his head. "I saw the sun shinin' off Reeve's badge, but not off'n the white man."

"He's got a white man with 'im?" Davis asked.

"He does."

"We gon' kill him, too?"

"We sure are," Private Edwards said. "Let's ride back a couple of miles. There was a likely place there for an ambush."

"We gonna back-shoot 'em?" Bush asked.

"We are," Edwards said. "We ain't takin' no chances with a hard man like Bass Reeves."

"Stop," Clint said.

"What?"

"Just hold up."

They reined their horses in.

"What's wrong?"

"I don't know," Clint said. "Something is. What's up ahead?"

"Lots of rocks."

"Anyplace where somebody could get above us?" Clint asked.

"Oh yeah. You sayin' somebody's layin' for us?" Reeves asked.

"Could be."

"How would you know that?"

"Come on, Bass," Clint said. "You've been doing this a long time."

"Instinct?"

Clint nodded, then touched his nose.

"I smell a rat."

Reeves stood in his stirrups and stared around, and then ahead of them.

"Whataya wanna do?" Reeves asked.

"I'll tell you . . ."

Edwards got himself situated up in some rocks. Across from him he saw Bush and Davis getting into position, also in some rocks. From this point they had a clear view of the ground below.

He could also look off into the distance and see one rider.

One rider.

It was Bass Reeves. The sun was still glinting off his badge.

But where was the white man?

He looked over at Bush and Davis again. From where they were, they could not see that Bass Reeves was riding alone.

Edwards looked around, couldn't see the white man anywhere.

He decided not to worry. He held his rifle in both hands. If he could get a clear shot at Deputy Bass Reeves, he could kill him, and then worry about where the white man went.

Bass Reeves's face was clear to Edwards now. He had seen the big black lawman before, and knew him on sight. He also didn't like him much, so he sighted down the barrel of his rifle, his finger hovering over the trigger, and waited.

ELEVEN

Bass Reeves saw one man up in the rocks, the sun reflecting off the metal of the man's rifle, or maybe a belt buckle or a spur. He assumed there were more because, after all, he and Clint were tracking more than one ex-Buffalo Soldier. If anything, they were across from him, so they'd be able to catch Reeves in a cross fire. That was exactly what a batch of Buffalo Soldiers would do.

He reined his horse in and waited. Clint needed time to get into position. At the moment, he was still out of range of anyone in those rocks with a rifle.

Or so he thought . . .

Private Luke Edwards was the best shot in the regiment while he was with the Buffalo Soldiers. He could make a shot with a Remington that no other man could make, the difference being the distance. While other soldiers needed to be closer, Edwards could make his shot from yards farther away.

He sighted down the barrel of his rifle, and fired.

Clint heard the shot. It had come way too soon. He was still climbing up the rock face, hoping to get behind the shooters so he could find out how many there were, maybe get the drop on them before anything could happen. Reeves was supposed to have remained out of range until then.

Clint started climbing faster.

Bush and Davis heard the shot, looked over at Edwards, saw him sighting down his barrel again. They looked, but they couldn't see what he was shooting at. Whoever it was was out of their sight, and range.

All they could do was wait.

The bullet grazed Reeves's shoulder. It wasn't much of a wound, but he made a show of falling from his horse. He lay still, figuring his next move. If the shooter believed he was dead, he might look away long enough for Reeves to move.

Edwards saw Reeves fall from his horse and land hard enough to kick up dust. He must have been dead. He looked over at Bush and Davis. They were staring at him, waiting for some kind of signal. He stood up to wave at them, then saw the man appear above his men. The white man. He must have climbed up from the back.

Edwards brought his rifle around and sighted along the barrel.

At this distance he couldn't miss . . .

Clint made it to the top and immediately saw the black man across from him. As the man raised his rifle, Clint drew and fired. His bullet struck the man in the chest. He dropped his rifle and fell to the ground below with an audible thud . . .

Bush and Davis saw Edwards fall, then looked above them to see the white man with the gun. He hadn't seen them yet.

They raised their rifles.

Bass Reeves came running up to the body of the fallen black man. A brief check of the man revealed him to be dead. He looked up and saw the other two black men, and Clint Adams. He quickly drew and began firing. He didn't have a clear shot, and his bullets bounced off rocks, but the sound alerted Clint.

Clint looked down at the sounds of the shots. He saw Reeves on the ground, and the two black men in the rocks. Reeves's shots had driven them to cover from below, but he could see them from above. He fired at them, but not to hit them. His bullets struck the rocks, peppering them with shards. As he'd hoped, the men reacted as if it was lead that was striking them, not stone chips.

They panicked.

* * *

Bush and Davis felt the rock shards striking them, thought they were bullets. They dropped their guns and began examining themselves for wounds. By the time they realized that neither had been shot, Clint had reloaded his gun.

"If I was you," he called out to them, "I'd climb down."

They stared up at him, then bent to retrieve their guns.

Clint fired once more, the bullet pinging off a rock very near them.

"Leave your guns where they are and climb down!" he called out.

Shoulders slumping in resignation, the two men began to climb down from the rocks.

Briefly, Clint wondered how he could climb down and keep the two men covered at the same time, but then he saw that Bass Reaves was right beneath them. He was sure the deputy would keep them covered while Clint worked his way down.

TWELVE

Bass Reeves was waiting for the two black men when they reached the ground. It took Clint a little longer to reach them.

Once they were all on the ground, Reeves said to them, "Your friend is dead."

They looked down at the dead man. All three of them were wearing Buffalo Soldier jackets with a single stripe.

"Take off those jackets!" Reeves commanded. "You're a disgrace to them."

"We earned these jackets, brother," Bush said to him.

"I ain't your brother," Reeves said. "And maybe you earned them once, but you don't deserve them now. Take 'em off!"

Slowly, the two men obeyed.

"Now take his off him," he said, indicating the dead man.

"He's dead," Davis said. "Why don't you leave him be?"

"Take the jacket off him," Reeves sad. "He didn't deserve it any more than you did."

Slowly, they crouched down by the body and removed his jacket. Then they handed all three jackets to Reeves. Meanwhile, Clint noticed Reeves had a slight wound on his left shoulder.

"Take a shot?" he asked, indicating the wound.

"He was a good shot, whoever he was," Reeves said. "He clipped me from a long ways off."

"How is it?"

"Not bad," Reeves said. "Where are your horses?" he asked the men.

"Same place mine is," Clint said. "I saw them when I started to climb."

"Okay," Reeves said, "we got to get their horses and yours and then we'll get goin'."

"Where?"

"We'll keep going to Muskogee," Reeves said, "And leave them in a cell there. Then we'll keep goin' till we catch the others."

"Maybe these fellas can help us with that," Clint suggested.

"Yeah," Reeves said, "we'll have to ask them. I'm sure they'll be happy to help."

They collected the horses, including the one that belonged to Private Edwards. Bush and Davis finally identified him for Reeves, which led the deputy to believe they might eventually cooperate.

They mounted up, tied the two live men to their saddles, and tossed Edwards over the back of his horse, trussed up so he wouldn't slide off.

"Anybody else up ahead waitin' to bushwack us?" Reeves asked them.

"We don't know," Davis said. "All we knew is what Edwards tol' us we was doin'."

"And what was that?"

"Killin' you."

"Were those your exact orders?"

"That's what Edwards said the sergeant wanted us to do," Bush said.

"Sergeant," Clint said. "Is that your commanding officer, or is there someone higher?"

"Nobody higher," Bush said. "Sergeant Washington gives the orders."

"Those raids and robberies you been pullin' have been his idea?"

"Yeah," Bush said, "he said it was time for us to start gettin' somethin' back."

"For what?" Clint asked. "Getting back for what?"

"For all the Buffalo Soldiers have done for the white man," Bush said.

"You feel entitled, then?" Clint asked.

"What's that mean?" Bush asked.

"You agree with your sergeant that the white man owes you something?"

"That's what the sergeant says," Davis said. "Why wouldn't it be true?"

Clint shook his head.

"The red man out here has got more coming to him than you do," Clint said.

All three black men, including Bass Reeves, looked at

him. Clint was certain that none of them agreed with what he'd just said.

"We better get movin'," Reeves said. "I wanna get these men to Muskogee."

"You gonna hang us?" Davis asked.

"That'll be up to Judge Parker," Reeves said, "I ain't gonna do nothin' but take you back. Ain't up to me to hang ya."

They rode on in a curious silence. Clint had a feeling he would hear from Reeves some time in the future about his opinions regarding white, black, and red men.

THIRTEEN

When they got to Muskogee, they stopped in to see Sheriff Overbay, the Cherokee lawman. They got the two black men installed in their cells and then Reeves made the introductions.

"This here's my friend Clint Adams," Reeves said to the lawman.

"Sam Overbay," the lawman said. "I heard of you." He put out his hand. Clint felt the man's power in his handshake, although he was sure the big Indian was taking it easy on him.

"We'll take this other fella over to the undertaker's," Reeves said.

"You gonna stay awhile?" Overbay asked.

"No," Reeves said. "We'll come back and question them two a little bit more, see if they can give us some idea where the others have gone. But we'll be ridin' out later today."

"I'll be here," Overbay said.

* * *

Clint and Bass Reeves left the sheriff's office, walked their horses as well as Edwards's horse over to the undertaker's with the body.

"What do you know about Sheriff Sam Overbay?" Clint asked.

"Not much," Reeves said. "He stayed out of my way last time I was here. I've never seen him have to do anything yet."

"Big man," Clint said.

"But that don't mean he can do nothin'," Reeves pointed out. "Size ain't everythin'."

When they carried the blanket-wrapped body into the undertaker's, the man looked at Bass Reeves and said, "You again."

They set the body on a table. The undertaker took a peek, then looked at Reeves again.

"Another black man?" he asked. "You like killin' your own kind?"

Reeves stared back at the undertaker, who was also black. He was an older man, his skin with that dusky, dry look old black men get.

"I'm doin' my job, old-timer," Reeves said. "Don't matter to me if they be black, white, or red. How about you?"

"Yeah, well . . ." the old man said. "Who's gonna pay?"

"Send a bill to Fort Smith, to Judge Parker," Reeves said. "He'll take care of it."

Clint and Reeves stepped outside.

"Don't let him bother you," Clint said. "He was out of line."

"He don't bother me none," Reeves said. "Come on, let's go ask them other two some questions."

"You think they're going to know where this Sergeant Washington took the others?"

"Maybe not," Reeves said. "Maybe he just sent them after me, figurin' he might lose 'em. But maybe they heard somethin' useful."

"Could be."

When they got to the sheriff's office, they went right into the cell blocks. The two men had been put in separate cells, but they were side by side. They were both lying on their bunks.

"Wake up! We got some questions for you two," Reeves said.

"We ain't got nothin' ta say to you, Reeves," Davis said.

"It might help you with Judge Parker if I can tell him you was cooperative," Reeves said.

The two men exchanged a glance between the bars.

"Well, whataya wanna know?" Bush asked.

"How many more of you are there disgracing the uniform?" Reeves asked.

"Well, suh," Bush said, "you done kilt three of us, and put us in here. That leaves . . . six?" He looked over at his partner.

"I ain't so good at sums," Davis said. "That sounds about right."

"Yeah, I think that leaves six," Bush said to Reeves with a nod.

"Where were they goin' when you split up?" Reeves asked.

"That we don't know," Davis said. "Maybe Edwards knew, but you done kilt him."

"We split up in groups of three after we left here," Bush said, still proving his ability with his sums. "But we don't know where they was goin'. Nobody never tol' us."

"Nobody tells us nothin'," the other man said.

"Even if you let us go," Davis said, "we wouldn't know where to go to join up with them again."

Reeves looked at Clint, who nodded, indicating he believed what they were saying.

"Okay," Reeves said.

He and Clint started to walk out.

"Hey, hey," Davis yelled, "you leavin' us here?"

"For a while," Reeves said. "But don't worry, we'll be back for you to take you see Judge Parker. You and the rest of your gang."

"We ain't a gang," Davis yelled, "we're a squad."

Reeves stopped halfway out the door and stepped in again, glaring at the men.

"You ain't no squad," he said. "You're a disgrace to the Buffalo Soldiers you used to serve in, but you don't no more. You're nothin' but a gang of outlaws, and I aim to bring you all in."

"Seems like you're aimin' to just kill us all," Bush said.

"Whether you go back dead or alive is up to all of you," Reeves said. "It don't make no never mind to me. But one way or another, you're going back."

Reeves left the cell blocks, ignoring whatever else the two black men had to say.

"How long you want me to hold 'em?" Sheriff Overbay asked.

"Until we get back," Bass Reeves said, "to pick 'em up."

"And what if you don't come back?"

"Oh, don't you worry, Sheriff," Reeves said. "We'll be back."

"Both of you?" Overbay asked.

"Yeah, both of us," Reeves said. "Just hold 'em for Judge Parker."

"Yes, sir," Overbay said.

As they left the office, Reeves asked, "Why would he think he should let them go at some point?"

"He's probably used to holdin' drunks for a day or two," Clint said. "I get the feeling he's not a real experienced lawman."

They walked their horses to the end of town the two black men indicated they had left by.

"Lots of tracks," Clint said. "How do we pick them out?"

"That's easy," Reeves said, getting down on one knee. "Look."

Clint looked down at the horseshoe print Reeves was pointing out.

"Wait," he said, "that's military issue."

"That's right," Reeves said. "These men still have their

jackets, and their military-issue horses. They really think they're still a Buffalo Soldier squad."

"They're deluded," Clint said. "And they feel they're owed."

"Well, maybe I ain't gonna give them what they're owed," Reeves said, "but I'm gonna give 'em what they got comin'."

"So then you are planning on killing them," Clint said.

Reeves looked at him.

"I don't lie to you, Clint," the black lawman said. "Not ever. If they make me kill 'em, I will. Otherwise I'm takin' em back to the Judge to let him do what he does best. That suit you?"

"Actually," Clint said, "that suits me just fine."

"Well, then," Reeves said, "I guess we better mount up and see where these tracks take us."

FOURTEEN

Sergeant Lemuel Washington was riding up ahead of his two men, alone with his thoughts—his thoughts being whether or not Edwards and the other two had been successful in trying to kill Bass Reeves, or if he'd managed to kill them instead.

He doubted it. Deputy Marshal Bass Reeves was a formidable man. It would probably take more than three men to kill him.

Private Franklin came riding up alongside him, interrupting his thoughts.

"Where we headed, Sarge?" he asked.

"Not to where anybody thinks we're headed, Private," Washington said.

"What's that mean?"

Washington looked at him.

"We're gettin' out of the Territories," he said. "We're gonna expand our operation."

"Expand it?"

"We're gonna spread out," Washington said. "Bass Reeves thinks he's gonna find us in the Territories. Well, he's gonna find out he's gonna have to go a lot farther to find us."

"But where we goin'?" the private asked.

"You'll see soon enough."

As Clint and Reeves put some distance between themselves and Muskogee, the tracks they were following separated into two groups.

They reined their mounts in, saw three sets of tracks going off to the north, and the other three continuing to the east.

"Split up?" Clint asked.

"If we'd split up earlier today," Reeves offered, "one of us would be dead."

"So what are you thinkin'?"

"I'm thinkin' maybe they split, but they're headed to the same place."

"So if we follow one set of three, they may lead us to the others eventually."

"Yeah, eventually."

"But who knows how long it will take," Clint said. He was still thinking that he had just been through this, and had been on the trail longer than he'd expected.

"Must be another way," he offered.

"Yeah, there is," Reeves said. "We catch up to one of these groups and they'll tell us where the other one is headed."

They mounted up.

"Okay," Clint said, "you're the man with the badge. Pick one."

"North," Reeves said.

"Maybe they're going to Kansas," Clint suggested. "Moving out of the Territories rather than have to deal with you."

"Goin' to Kansas ain't gonna solve that for 'em," Reeves said. "They're gonna have to deal with me—and you, no matter what."

They rode in silence for a while and then Clint asked, "What do you suppose their aim would be in going to Kansas?"

Reeves seemed to give the question some thought before responding.

"Well, like you said, maybe they don't think I'd follow them," he said, rubbing his jaw thoughtfully. "Or maybe they're just tryin' to spread out themselves out some. They're ex-military, their sergeant must have a plan."

"I'm thinking he's got a target in mind," Clint said. "Someplace in Kansas that he's going to hit. If we knew what and where that was, we could be there waiting for them."

"There's no way to figure that one out, is there?" Reeves said. "We're just gonna have to keep followin' them."

"I was afraid you'd say that."

FIFTEEN

Franklin rode up to Washington and said, "We's in Kansas."

"Yes, we are."

"You know where we're goin', don't ya?" Franklin asked.

"I heard some things last week, when we ran into those boys," Washington said.

"The ones we killed and robbed 'cause they had just hit a bank?"

"That's right," Washington said. "They told me about a bank in a town called Kilkenny."

"A big bank?"

"Not a big one," Washington said, "but a rich one."

"Can the three of us hit it?"

"Don't you worry about that," Washington said. "I got that part taken care of, too."

The man looked at his leader, then looked back at the other rider.

"We's wonderin', that's all."

"Well," Washington said, "stop wonderin' and just follow me. Understand?"

"Yessuh."

Franklin rode back to explain what he'd learned to
Gordon.

They stopped at the border.

"Kansas," Clint said.

Reeves stood in his stirrups and looked around.

"At least we won't have to watch out for Indians," Clint
said.

"We ain't had no trouble with Indians," Reeves
reminded him.

"I know it," Clint said, "I was just trying to look on
the bright side."

"Ain't no bright side to this, Clint," Reeves said. "I get
the feelin' these men ain't gonna come easy."

"That won't make the Judge happy."

"I ain't so worried about the Judge," the black deputy
said. "Me and him got a understandin'."

"And that is?"

"Sometimes," he said, "folks just don't wanna come
in alive."

SIXTEEN

Clint and Reeves were getting ready to make camp for the night when they saw lights up ahead.

"You been up to this corner of the Territories before?" Clint asked.

"A few times, but I ain't usually crossed in Kansas here," Reeves explained, "so I don't know what town that is."

They hadn't come across any town signposts. Also, the tracks they were following did not lead directly to those lights. They skirted around them.

"If the Soldiers passed here in daylight, they might not have seen that town," Clint suggested. "Or they deliberately bypassed it."

"If it's a town at all," Reeves said. "All we see are some lights."

"Well," Clint said, "there's only one way to find out."

Reeves hesitated.

"If it's a town, it's better than camping and having beef jerky again," Clint pointed out.

"Okay," Reeves said, "we'll ride over there and check it out."

It was a town.

That much they could tell when they rode in. It wasn't much of a town, and they didn't see a town name anywhere, but the lights were real lights in real windows and—best of all—they could smell food.

They found a saloon, which looked like it was the place throwing out the most light.

"This is probably the place we saw from a distance," Reeves said, dismounting.

They stepped up onto the boardwalk and started for the batwings. Clint put his hand on Bass Reeves's arm to stop him.

"What?"

"How about taking the badge off?"

"What?"

"Put it in your pocket," Clint said. "It's just a suggestion. Let's not look for trouble when we don't know what we're walking into."

Clint could see Reeves was struggling with the suggestion, but finally the black man took the badge off and put it in his shirt pocket.

They stepped through the batwings.

It was a small saloon, brightly lit and noisy, with girls working the floor. It was remarkably lively for a small-town place that apparently had no gambling and no music.

They walked to the bar, watched blatantly by most of the men in the place.

"I guess they don't get many strangers here," Clint said.

"You might've been right about the badge," Reeves admitted.

They got to the bar, made room for the both of them, and ordered a cold beer each.

"Did you notice a name on the front of the saloon?" Clint asked Reeves.

"No saloon name, and no town name," Reeves said.

"They must be trying to keep this place a secret. Either that or there are signs all over the place that we can't see in the dark."

Reeves called the bartender over.

"Yeah?" The bartender was a middle-aged white man with a heavy beard. He was giving Bass Reeves a hard look. There were no other black men in the place.

"What town are we in?"

"Poison Springs."

"What?"

The man looked at Clint.

"You hard of hearin'?"

"Why would anyone name their town Poison . . . anything?"

"Look, friend, I just work here."

He walked away.

"Not very friendly," Clint said.

"That's because of me," Reeves said. "I been gettin' those looks since we walked in."

"Well, there's a cure for that."

"What's that?"

"Put the badge back on," Clint said.

"But you said—"

"I know what I said," Clint replied, cutting him off, "but I'd love to see everyone's reaction when you put it on."

Reeves thought about it a moment, then shrugged, took the badge out, and pinned it back on.

The bartender was the first one to see it. He stared at the tin, then looked at Reeves's face again. Reeves didn't react.

Then Reeves picked up his beer mug and turned his back to the bar. That gave everyone in the saloon a clear look at the badge. In that moment Clint was almost jealous—almost wished he himself had a badge he could take out and pin on.

SEVENTEEN

There were a lot of big black men in the West, but when you saw a big black man wearing a deputy marshal's badge, it was Bass Reeves.

"Bass Reeves," somebody said, and the saloon got quieter.

"Here ya go, Deputy Reeves," the bartender said. "A nice fresh beer."

Reeves turned and looked at the man.

"I ain't finished this one," he said, "and by the time I do, that one'll be warm."

"Yeah, okay, sorry," the man said, taking the beer back. "Just let me know when yer done and I'll let ya have another one . . . on the house."

"And for my friend," Reeves said.

"Huh? Oh, yeah, sure," the bartender said, "one fer your friend."

Clint thought Reeves was going to say his name, and

was happy when he didn't. No point in letting all the cats out of their bags.

"I'm lookin' for three or six more black men," Reeves said, "You seen 'em?"

"Three, or six?"

"That's right. Seen 'em?"

The bartender shook his head.

"If they passed by, they didn't bother to stop here, Deputy," the man said. "I swear. You can ask anybody. This ain't a big town, and that many black men would be noticed."

Clint knew he was right.

"Yeah," Reeves said, finishing his beer. He set the empty mug on the bar. "I'm finished." He looked at Clint. "You finished?"

"Yeah," Clint said, setting his mug down, "I'm finished."

"Two more," the bartender said. "Yes, sir, comin' up."

He went off to draw the beers.

"Whataya think?" Reeves asked.

"Seems to me he's telling the truth," Clint said.

"Yeah, me, too."

"We could ask a few of the others, but it probably doesn't matter."

"Let's get somethin' to eat," Reeves said, "and then a room."

"Right."

"Each," Reeves said, "a room each."

"Suits me," Clint said.

They both liked their privacy. Clint liked to read in the privacy of his own room. He didn't know what Reeves liked.

                      *   *   *

They were finishing their beers when one of the saloon girls came up next to Reeves, looking him up and down. She was pretty enough, looked to be experienced—late twenties, or early thirties—was tall and blond.

She licked her lips and smiled at Reeves.

"Are you really Bass Reeves?"

"Yes, ma'am."

"You're big."

"Yes, ma'am."

"Are you big . . . all over?"

Deputy Reeves frowned, not sure what she was asking him.

"Ma'am . . . I think so."

She laughed, ran her hand over his chest, and said, "You're cute."

"Oh, I don't think that's true, ma'am," he said, shaking his head.

"Are you stayin' in town overnight?" she asked.

"Yes, ma'am."

"Well, Mister Reeves," she said, "I guess I'll be seein' you later."

She moved away from him, back onto the floor to do her job. Reeves turned to Clint, looking confused. Clint didn't know quite how much experience Bass Reeves had with women—or with saloon girls.

"Don't worry," Clint said. "You'll get it."

While the blonde had been sizing up Reeves, the brunette saloon girl had been watching Clint from across the room.

She was shorter, younger, more full-bodied than her blond counterpart. Clint returned her look, toasted her with his beer mug. She smiled, ran her finger along the cleft formed by her chubby breasts.

"I guess we better get some rooms," Reeves said, setting his empty mug down on the bar. "We gotta get an early start in the mornin'."

Clint nodded, drained his own mug, and placed it on the bar.

"More, Deputy?" the bartender asked.

"No, that's enough," Reeves said. "You got a lawman in this town?"

The bartender fidgeted a bit, then said, "Well, sort of."

"What's that mean?"

"You gonna talk to him?"

Reeves nodded, said, "In the mornin'."

"Then you'll find out for yourself," the bartender said, "he ain't much of a lawman."

"As long as he's wearin' a badge," Reeves said.

"Oh, he wears one," the barman said. "But he ain't gonna be much good to you."

"Like you said," Reeves replied, "I'll find out for myself."

Clint and Reeves left the saloon. As soon as they were gone, the bartender's expression changed to one of naked hatred. He looked over at a table of three men and beckoned them to come over.

"What's up?" one asked.

"I got a job for you . . ."

EIGHTEEN

They left the saloon and took their horses to the livery. They had to wake the man to take the horses in. He gave Reeves a dirty look until he saw that badge. Then his attitude changed.

"Would you be Bass Reeves?" he asked.

"I would."

"And judging from this horse," the man went on, "you're the Gunsmith."

"You know that from my horse?"

"Fella," the man said, "I'm eighty years old." Clint thought he looked abut sixty. "I've seen a lot over the course of my life. I can usually make a good guess about who a body is."

"Then maybe you can guess the location of about half a dozen black men, ex-Buffalo Soldiers," Clint said. "Been seen in the area?"

"Not here," the man said, "but they did pass by, on their way . . . somewhere."

"Like where?"

"North."

"That's it?"

The man shrugged.

"They were headin' north when they passed here a couple of days ago," he said. "After that they could've went . . . anywhere. That helpful?"

"Not a lot," Reeves said.

"But I still get to look after your horse for one night, right?" he asked Clint.

"Right." Clint handed him Eclipse's reins. "And he better be here and happy when I come back tomorrow morning."

"Don't worry," the man said. "I wouldn't do anything to a magnificent beast like this."

"And mine?" Reeves asked.

"I'll see to him, too."

Reeves handed his reins over.

"What can you tell us about the lawman you got in town?" Reeves asked.

"You ain't gonna get much help out of him," the old man said.

"Why not?"

"He's only wearin' it because nobody else wanted it," the liveryman said.

"But he does his job, doesn't he?" Reeves asked.

The man shrugged.

"I guess we will have to find out for ourselves in the morning, like the bartender said."

"This town might as well not have a lawman at all.

The bartender knows what he's talkin' about," the livery-man said.

"That a fact?" Reeves asked.

The man nodded.

"He learned from me," he said. "He's my son."

"That a fact?"

The liveryman nodded.

"My oldest."

Considering the way the man had looked at him when they entered the stable, Reeves said, "Why doesn't that surprise me?"

"You got a hotel in this town?" Clint asked.

"Poison Springs Hotel," the man said. "Only one in town."

"Clean?" Clint asked.

"Does that matter?" the man asked. "I said it's the only one in town."

"Right."

"Can you tell us how this town got named Poison Springs?" Reeves asked.

"Oh, that's simple," the man said. "At the time, I couldn't think of anything else to call it."

NINETEEN

They checked into the hotel, which had plenty of rooms, so they were able to get one each. They carried their rifles and saddlebags upstairs.

"You see that desk clerk?" Clint asked in the hall. They had gotten rooms right across from each other.

Reeves nodded.

"Heavy beard, beady eyes."

"What do you want to bet he's another son?"

"Family-owned town," Reeves said. "I hope this wasn't a bad idea."

"Too late now," Clint said. "Let's get some sleep and get out of here in the morning."

"After breakfast," Reeves said. "I want a hot breakfast."

"Agreed."

"Night, Clint."

"See you in the morning."

Clint opened the door to his room and went inside. He heard Reeves's door close.

* * *

It was a couple of hours later when Clint heard the sound of someone walking down the hall. The walking stopped and then he heard a knock—but not at his door.

He grabbed his gun from the holster on the bedpost—a tried-and-true place to keep his gun when he was in a hotel room—and padded barefoot to the door. He cracked the door open enough to look out. He saw the blond girl from the saloon standing at Reeves's door. At that moment she knocked again, and the door opened.

Reeves appeared in the doorway, bare-chested and barefoot.

"What—" he said.

She quieted him by putting her hand against his bare chest and rubbing it.

"Oh my," she said. She pushed him and he stepped back. She entered and closed the door behind her.

Clint closed his door quietly, returned his gun to his holster, and resumed his position on the bed. He picked up the book he had been reading.

The saloon girl was about to find out if Bass Reeves was that big all over.

A short time later Clint again heard the sound of footsteps in the hall. They stopped, and the knock came on his door.

He grabbed the gun once again, padded to the door, and opened it. It was the other girl from the saloon, the brunette with the chubby breasts.

"Surprised to see me?" she asked. "I thought we were sending each other messages across the room."

"We were," Clint said. "Come in."

He backed away from the door to admit her, once again returned his gun to his holster.

"What made you think you'd need that?" she asked. "You must have known I was coming."

"But how did I know you'd come alone?"

"Oh, handsome," she said, "I wouldn't want to share you with anybody. Besides, the only other person I might have brought was Letty, and isn't she across the hall with your big black friend?"

"I suppose she is."

"Want to go and listen at the door?"

"No, thanks," Clint said. "He may have kicked her out."

"I haven't met a man yet who would kick her out of bed."

She dropped her shawl to the floor. She was still wearing her saloon dress, cut low to reveal creamy shoulders and lots of equally creamy breast.

"Or me," she added.

"I can believe that."

"What?" she asked with a smirk.

"What you just said."

"I want to hear you say it, handsome."

"I can believe that no man has ever kicked you out of bed."

"Show me," she said. "Show me how you believe it."

He walked to the door.

"Are you leaving?" she asked. "Have I frightened you away?"

"No," he said. "I just want to make sure the door is locked."

He turned the key and locked it, then pressed on the door. It wasn't a good one. One good kick would splinter it open.

"Are we ready?" she asked.

He turned, saw her standing there with her dress down around her ankles.

"You are," he said.

She put her hands on her hips and said, "I'll wait."

TWENTY

In the lobby the bartender entered with three other men from the saloon.

"What are you doin' here?" his brother, the desk clerk, asked.

"Did that big black bastard with the badge check in?" the bartender asked.

"Yeah, he's in room five," the desk clerk said. "His friend is in six."

"Bass Reeves, right?" the bartender asked.

"That's right."

"Well, get your gun," the bartender said. "That black bastard made a fool of me and I ain't about to stand for it."

"What about his friend?" the desk clerk asked.

"I don't care about the friend," the bartender insisted.

"I think you better care about him."

"Why?"

His brother reversed the register and said, "Look for yourself."

The bartender read the name on the register, then turned to the three men with him.

"We're gonna need more guns."

While Clint undressed slowly, he asked, "What's your name?"

"Julie."

"Don't you have any men in town you like, Julie?" he asked.

"It's the fact that you're a stranger that makes you appeal to me," she said. "When we're done, you'll leave town, and I won't have to deal with you."

"That sounds like something a man would say," he commented.

"Men aren't so wrong about everything," she told him. "Just most things. Ooh."

She said "ooh" when he dropped his pants and underwear and she saw his cock, already coming to life.

She came to him on strong legs, her thighs as juicy and rounded as her breasts, and took hold of him, stroking him. He reached behind to grab her buttocks, found them as full as the rest of her. The woman was perfectly built for bouncing around on a bed. He just wished they had a better bed to bounce around on.

And a better town to do it in.

But before they got to the bed, she fell to her knees before him and took him into her mouth, sucking him avidly, wetly.

"Oh my God," she whispered, as if actually speaking to his cock. "You're so beautiful."

She took him in, wet him fully, and then slid him out, stroking him with her hand.

Clint had backed them toward the bed, meaning to put her on it, but also so he'd be closer to his gun.

Just in case . . .

The bartender and the desk clerk were brothers, Mike and Mark McCall. They had three men each following them up the stairs, so the staircase was a little crowded, and objecting in the form of loud creaking.

"Easy," Mike hissed at the men. "Go single file, for Chrissake!"

The men had been trying to get up the stairs at the same time. Now they backed off and went single file behind the two brothers.

"I want that black marshal," Mike the bartender said. "He's mine."

"Okay," his brother said, "we'll take Adams."

They stopped at the top of the stairs and turned to the other men.

"We got to go quiet!" he hissed.

The men all nodded, and then they started down the hall.

Clint had had many women come to his room, for various reasons. A lot of them came for sex. Women liked him, and he thought it was because he treated them well, made them feel good. He always felt a man and a woman should both come out of their shared time happy and satisfied.

But there was another reason women came to his room, and it was one that had happened to him just weeks ago. Women had been sent to his room to keep him busy while someone tried to kill him.

He hadn't liked the way the men in the saloon had looked at them, especially the bartender. If they had sent these two women up to keep them busy, they'd be sneaking down the hall just about now. Which would explain the creaking noises he'd heard. He'd noticed the stairs creaking when he and Reeves had used them.

Still on her knees, moaning with her mouth full, Julie slid her hands up the backs of his thighs until she reached his buttocks, then clutched them and pulled him to her as she took his cock all the way down her throat. He hoped she wasn't setting him up, because she was very good at this and he would have liked very much for her to finish . . .

But then he heard the floorboards . . .

Bass Reeves lifted the blond girl off him and got to his feet.

"Get down behind the bed," he told her. "Or maybe under it."

"But what—"

"Just do it!"

Her eyes were glassy. Standing there naked, he looked like a statue made of smooth black marble. She reached for him, wanting him in her again, but he pushed her hand away and said, "Get behind the bed and stay down!"

She did as he said, her eyes beginning to focus again.

She didn't know why he was pushing her down behind the bed, but she could guess.

He grabbed his gun and stood against the wall, behind the door, held his fingers to his lips. She thought he looked absolutely beautiful like that . . .

TWENTY-ONE

When the door slammed open, Clint did two things: he pushed Julie out of the way, and drew his gun from the holster on the bedpost.

Four men came pouring into the room led by the desk clerk. They all had guns in their hands, but they all had to look around a moment to locate Clint, while he could plainly see them coming through the door. He started shooting first . . .

The door to Bass Reeves's door slammed open, barely missing him as it slammed into the wall. The girl on the floor screamed and tried her best to get under the bed.

As the four men came through the door, led by the bartender, Reeves grabbed the door and slammed it back on them. It struck two of the men, causing them to stagger back into the hall.

The first two looked around the room wildly, trying to locate Reeves. When they saw him, they froze. Naked, holding his gun, he had the look of a gladiator from times gone by. He was a fearsome sight.

"Big mistake, friend," he said to the bartender . . .

Clint fired, put two bullets in the chest of the desk clerk. The bearded man fell to the floor, causing the man behind him to trip. Clint shot him while he was falling, killing him.

The trailing two men realized something bad was happening in the room, and tried to reverse course. This wasn't worth the twenty dollars they were being paid.

Clint followed them into the hall, still naked, and fired at them as they tried to escape. They fired back, but their shots went wild, and in seconds they were lying on the floor of the hall, dead.

Doors began to open, and there were still shots, these coming from Bass Reeves's room . . .

The bartender and the second man turned, their eyes wide as they saw Reeves, and they tried to bring their guns to bear. But Bass Reeves had not stated the matter clearly enough. It was not only a bad idea, but a decidedly deadly one.

"Wait—" the bartender yelled, but it was too late. Reeves killed him and the second man just as the third and fourth men got the door open again and came running into the room.

When they saw the naked black man with the gun, they stopped and one of them said, "Whoa!"

That was way too late. They knew Reeves was going

to fire. One man squeezed his eyes shut so he wouldn't see it coming. The other man tried to bring his gun around. Neither man had chosen the right course of action, and in seconds they were both dead.

Reeves heard the shots in the hall, and rushed for the door . . .

Clint saw Reeves come rushing from his room after the last shot, and now he and the black deputy marshal were standing there, naked, brandishing guns.

Reeves looked up and down the hall, saw people peering out of their rooms, and shouted, "Back inside!"

They withdrew their heads and shoulders and slammed their doors.

"Have you got a girl in your room, Bass?" Clint asked him.

"Yeah, I do," Bass Reeves said, "the blond saloon girl."

"Yeah, I got the brunette," Clint said. "I'll bring her into your room. Let's find out if they were in on this."

"Right."

Reeves went back into his room and got Letty out from under the bed. By that time Clint had dragged the naked brunette into the room. There was a lot of smooth, pale skin in evidence. Clint had taken the time to pull on his pants, so Reeves did the same. Now the skin that was showing was mostly female.

There was some commotion in the hall now that Clint and Reeves were not there. Clint slammed the door of Reeves's room. It wouldn't close firmly, but it stayed just ajar.

"Are you ladies aware what just happened?" Clint asked.

"No," Letty said. "I—I was under the bed."

Clint looked at Julie.

"Seems to me you killed some men who were tryin' to kill you."

"And is that what you'll tell the sheriff?" Clint asked.

She smirked and said, "Well, yeah, but it won't matter much."

"Why not?"

"Because he ain't much of a sheriff."

"You let us worry about that," Reeves said. "What we wanna know now is, what—if anythin'—did you two know about this?"

"Wha—" Letty said.

"God, no!" Julia said. "You think if I knew lead was gonna be flying, I'd be here?"

Clint studied her. She didn't look as frightened as her friend, Letty, but both girls looked to him to be telling the truth.

"You gals better get dressed," he told the naked women. "We're probably going to be having some company soon."

Letty grabbed her clothes, and she and Julie ran to Clint's room to get dressed.

"You believe them?" Reeves asked.

"Yeah, I do," Clint said, scratching his head. "There was too much of a chance of them getting hurt for them to be in on it."

"I guess you're right."

"Too bad," Clint said. "I was sort of having a good time."

"When did you realize what was happenin'?" the black deputy asked.

"Oh," Clint said, "I had an idea that even if they weren't in on it, somebody might use them as a distraction anyway. I didn't like the looks we were getting in the saloon. I think I know why the town is called Poison Springs. It's not exactly friendly."

"Did it ever occur to you to warn me?" Reeves asked his friend.

"Oh, I knew you'd hear them coming down the hall like a herd of cattle," Clint said.

"Yeah, well," Reeves said, "you better go get dressed if the sheriff's comin'."

"And then we'll get our rooms changed," Clint suggested.

"Why bother?" Reeves asked. "Let's just saddle up and get out of here before somethin' else happens."

Clint shrugged.

"That suits me."

•

TWENTY-TWO

When the sheriff arrived, they learned firsthand that Julie had been right. The lawman was bleary-eyed and smelled of booze. He looked around at the dead men on the floor of the rooms and the hall and said, "Looks like self-defense to me."

Clint and Reeves didn't object. The sheriff got some men to remove the dead bodies, and then he went back to whatever he had been doing—sleeping, drinking, probably both.

The girls left, as well, and when they were alone, Clint and Reeves collected their saddlebags and rifles and walked to the livery.

As they approached the front doors, there were a couple of shots, and two bullets dug into the dirt in front of them. Both men stopped, but didn't take cover. Clint knew what was happening.

"Shit," Reeves said.

"What?"

"That bartender and desk clerk. They were his sons."

"I forgot about that," Clint said. "I guess he heard the news."

"Hello, the stable!" Reeves called out.

"Yeah, I'm here!" the man called back. "And I got your horse, Adams. I'm gonna kill it."

Clint felt a moment of panic, then remembered the look on the man's face when he handed over the reins. This was a man who loved horses—especially good ones.

"He ain't gonna kill that horse," Reeves said. "Not even for revenge."

"I figured," Clint said. "He thinks too much of horses."

"Then what do we do? Wait him out?"

"We're out in the open," Clint said. "He could have killed us easily. He chose to fire warning shots. His heart ain't in it."

"Then what do we do? Just walk in?"

"No," Clint said after a moment, "that would tempt him."

There was another shot, this one landing in the dirt closer to them. It was dark, but there was enough of a moon to light them up as targets.

"Let's start by getting back into the shadows," Clint suggested.

They backed up until they reached the building across the way, a feed and grain store. It was two stories high, and threw a long, dark shadow.

"Now what?" Reeves asked,

"You keep him talking," Clint said. "I'll work my way around the back."

"Okay. You gonna kill 'im?"

"Not if I can help it," Clint said. "I think we've killed enough members of his family for one night, don't you?"

When Clint got around to the back of the stable, he could hear the man inside and Reeves exchanging words, but he couldn't make out what they were saying. That didn't matter. Once he got inside, he could stop the man from talking, and shooting.

He found the single back door. It was unlocked. He stepped inside, drew his gun. There was a lamp burning, and he could see the man standing by the front door with his rifle. He could also see Eclipse in one of the stalls.

He moved up behind the man and said, "Put the rifle down, friend."

The man froze. If he turned, Clint would have to shoot him. Instead, he simply stood still.

"You killed my boys."

"They tried to kill us."

"Might as well kill me, then."

"Not unless you turn on me with that rifle," Clint sad. "Now put it down."

The man didn't move.

"There's no point to this," Clint sad.

"No point in livin' without my boys."

"Look," Clint said, "we both know you could have shot us outside, and if you were really ready to die, you would have turned on me by now. So put . . . the rifle . . . down!"

The man hesitated, then dropped the rifle.

"Bass! It's okay to come in!" Clint shouted.

The man turned and walked to the side, sat down on a bale of hay. Bass Reeves opened the front doors and walked in.

"Okay?"

"That's his rifle."

Reeves picked it up, unloaded it, and tossed it aside.

"Let's get out of here before somebody else gets it in their heads to kill us," he said.

"Right."

They saddled their horses and walked them outside. The liveryman—whose name they never learned—remained where he was, staring at the ground between his feet.

They mounted up, looked back at him.

"I'm sorry," Clint said.

The man didn't respond. Clint and Reeves exchanged a look, then rode out of Poison Springs.

TWENTY-THREE

A few miles outside of town they stopped to camp and get some sleep. They were both starving. They had gotten to town too late to get something to eat, and had to leave town without having breakfast. Clint put on a pot of coffee and they ate what beef jerky they had left.

"That's the last time I stop in any town that has the word 'Poison' in the name."

"We better stand watch tonight," Reeves said. "Those crazies might come after us."

Clint nodded. They drank coffee and ate while they discussed what they had to do the next day.

"We're going to have to pick up some supplies in the next town," Clint said.

"Let's hope it's not a town of crazy people, like the last one," Reeves said.

"When it gets light, I'll have to find their trail again," Clint said. "Lucky their horses are wearing those Army horseshoes."

"Seems like they kept everythin' from the Buffalo Soldiers except the spirit," Reeves lamented.

"That disappoints you."

Reeves looked at Clint.

"I feel odd," he said, "like somebody close to me died."

"I understand," Clint said. "Your time with the Buffalo Soldiers was special. Maybe it was special to these men, too, at one time, but now they've got something eating at them inside that you don't."

"I ain't forgot what my people had to go through," Reeves said. "I get real angry and bitter sometimes, but these men . . . men I might have called brothers once . . . they're givin' my people a bad name. They're givin' folks somethin' to point to and say, 'See? They nothin' but animals.'"

"Well, I want to say I understand, Bass," Clint said, "but I guess there's no way I could. But I do sympathize with you."

"I appreciate it," Reeves said. He picked up the coffeepot, found it empty. "I'll make another pot and take first watch."

"Okay."

Clint wrapped himself in his blanket, put his head on his saddle, and set his holster right next to his head. He didn't think people from town would be coming after them, but who knew? They had been forced to kill six townsmen, and the law hadn't done anything about it. All they needed was a bunch of vigilantes with torches and a rope to find them asleep in camp.

Even though Reeves was on watch, Clint didn't sleep

very well, and was already awake when Reeves nudged him four hours later.

Clint made still another pot of coffee as the sun came up, the last pot they'd be able to make until they bought some supplies in the next town.

He handed Reeves a cup as he woke him. The big black man rolled to his feet readily, appearing to be fully awake.

"I think we should swing east," Reeves said. "If our men circled the town, maybe we'll pick up their trail out there."

"Up to you," Clint said. "I can usually hold my own as a tracker, but with you, I'll gladly follow."

They broke camp, stomped the fire, and saddled their horses.

They came to a signpost that said: KILKENNY, KANSAS.

"We coulda stopped in Coffeyville, got some hot food," Gordon grumbled.

"And a hot woman," Franklin added.

"With the money we're gonna make in Kilkenny," Washington said from ahead of them, "you can get all the food and women you want, hot or cold."

They looked at each other, always amazed at what that man could say.

Washington turned in his saddle and looked at them both.

"You boys wanna ride back to Coffeyville, be my guest," he said.

"Naw," Gordon said, "that's okay, Sarge."

"We're with you," Franklin said.

"All right," Washington said. "No more complaints, then."

"Yessir," Franklin said.

"Yeah, right," Gordon agreed.

Washington turned and looked at the sign again. No population numbers. He didn't like that. He hoped the information he'd gotten about Kilkenny was right.

"Let's go," he said.

TWENTY-FOUR

"Coffeyville?" Reeves asked.

"Independence after that," Clint said.

"The tracks are still goin' north," Reeves said. "I think they're gonna bypass both towns."

"And go where?" Clint asked. "What town around here's got a big enough strike for them—Wichita?"

"Dodge City?"

"There's nothing in Dodge anymore," Clint said. "In the old days any of these towns would have a bank with cattle money in it. Wichita, Ellsworth, Dodge . . . but not now."

"Then maybe it's not money," Reeves said.

"What do you mean?"

"They been killin' people," Reeves said.

"You think they're looking for someplace to kill . . . who? A dignitary? Or just a lot of people?"

"Or both."

"All right, then," Clint said. "We keep going."

"I never thought anything else," Bass Reeves said.

Corporal Jefferson accepted a beer from Carl Weatherby, who then handed another to Ben Webster.

"Siddown, Carl," Jefferson said.

Weatherby sat with his own beer.

"They shoulda been here by now, Corporal," Weatherby said.

"Don't worry, Carl," Jefferson said. "The sarge will be here. He gave us the short way so we'd be here waitin' for him."

"Well," Carl Weatherby said, "I'm getting' tired of waitin'."

"Then go back upstairs," Jefferson said. "I'll bet you ain't wore out that whore yet."

Weatherby brightened and said, "That's a good idea." He stood, holding his beer, and looked at Webster. "She got a sister."

Webster smiled and stood up. "You don't gotta ask me twice."

They both looked at their corporal, and Weatherby said, "Sorry, Corporal, she ain't got a mother."

"Get outta here before I put you both on sentry duty," he growled.

The two younger men laughed and carried their beers up the stairs to the second floor.

Jefferson sat alone, not bothering to look around him. He knew what he'd see. Tables of white faces, glaring at him. He didn't care. He was used to the white man's hatred. He had enough black man's hatred to give right back to them, but he held it in check. If they hated him now, wait until he and Washington and the rest of the men got through with this town.

He finished his beer and decided to walk around town. Although Sergeant Washington had told him their next job was in Kilkenny, Jefferson still didn't know exactly what the job was. He was going to walk around town and try to guess, maybe stop someplace and get something to eat.

And hope to stay out of trouble.

Washington led the way, with Gordon and Franklin riding behind him. Jefferson was the only one of his men who he really talked to. The corporal was older than he was, and Washington made as much use as possible of the man's experience.

But the other men had to look to him as the leader, so the only time he spoke to them was to tell them what to do. He never asked for advice, or comments. Their job was to just follow orders.

And not question him.

Gordon and Franklin rode behind Washington, wondering what the man had on his mind. They also wondered where Edwards, Bush, and Davis were, if they were going to meet them in Kilkenny along with Jefferson and the others.

"I still don't think we been doin' the right things, Gordo," Franklin said.

"What you wanna do, then?"

"I think you and me gotta go out on our own," Franklin said. "Get our own business done."

"You really think we can do better that way?"

"Don't nobody ask us what we think," Franklin said, "ever. I would like to be treated like I was a man, just once."

"Yeah, but"—he lowered his voice—"Washington is the sergeant, ya'll . . ."

"Well, that's another thing," Franklin said. "Gordo, man, we ain't even in the Buffalo Soldiers no more. We just wearin' the jackets."

"Keep your voice down," Gordon said. "He hears us talkin' about goin' out on our own and he'll kill us."

"And I don't need to be afraid that no man's gonna kill me if'n I say somethin' he don't like," Franklin said. "I swear, Gordo, this should be our last job with him."

Gordon didn't know what to think, but he was glad when Franklin finally quieted down.

TWENTY-FIVE

Clint and Reeves stopped to rest the horses. Actually, they stopped to rest Bass Reeves's horse. Clint's Darley Arabian could have gone on all day, and Reeves knew it.

"That damn horse of yours don't never get tired, does he?" the big black man asked.

"I've never gotten to the bottom of him," Clint said. "Not yet. I don't even know if he has a bottom."

Reeves stroked his horse's neck and spoke to him, telling him not to be intimidated by Eclipse.

"You think he understands you?" Clint asked.

"No, he don't," Reeves said. "He ain't like your horse, but I figure I'll talk to him anyway."

They drank from their canteens, hung them back on their saddles, and mounted up.

"We'll ride awhile longer and then camp," Reeves said. "We'll make Kilkenny by tomorrow afternoon."

"Hopefully," Clint said, "we'll find what we're looking for when we get there."

* * *

Jefferson stood across the street from the bank, watching. It didn't look like they did much of a business—at least not people walking in. It was a small building, probably had a small safe. This could not be the next job that Washington had been talking about. There had to be something else.

He kept walking.

Washington halted their progress by raising his gloved hand. Gordon and Franklin rode up on either side of him and reined in.

"Where are we?" Gordon asked.

"Kilkenny is over that rise," Washington said.

"That's where we're goin', ain't it?" Franklin asked.

"Yeah," Washington said, "that's where we're goin'."

"What's the job?" Gordon asked. "What's there?"

"You'll see," Washington said. "You'll both see when we get there."

"Are we goin'?" Gordon asked. "Now?"

"In a minute," Washington said, dismounting. "I want to rest my horse."

"Now?" Franklin asked.

"Yes, now."

He walked his horse away from the two men, started checking his saddle, made sure the cinch was tight, let the horse take a breather—and looked behind them. As far as he could see, there was nobody there—but there was. He knew there was.

Bass Reeves was there.

He wondered what Reeves would think when he saw him.

"Bass?"

"Yes?"

"Can you think of anyone who would do this?" Clint asked. "Any Buffalo Soldier you ever knew who might use his training, and his men, to do something like this?"

They were riding along at an easy pace, side by side, probably less than an hour from stopping for the night.

"I been thinkin' about that," Reeves said. "Askin' myself the same question."

"You come up with an answer?"

"No," Reeves said. "The Soldiers I knew were honest, decent men."

"No angry men?"

Reeves smiled tightly.

"We're black men, Clint," he said. "We're all angry."

"Even you?"

"I said 'we,'" Reeves answered.

Clint let the subject go.

They camped. All they had left was some water in their canteens, and a few pieces of beef jerky. They had not stopped in any town to restock.

"If they're not in Kilkenny," Clint said, "we'll have to do some shopping."

"Then we will," Reeves said. "We'll keep huntin' until we catch 'em."

"What about Judge Parker?"

"What about him?"

"Won't he wonder where you are?"

"No," Reeves said. "If his deputies are not in town, he assumes they are out doin' their jobs."

"You could send him a telegram, tell him where we are, what we're doing."

"He would wonder why I am doin' that," Reeves said. "No, there's no need."

"What if one of his deputies never comes back?" Clint asked.

"He assumes they are dead."

"Without proof?"

"The fact that they didn't come back is all the proof he needs."

"I guess . . ."

After a few minutes Reeves said, "Can I ask you a question?"

"Sure."

"How many times has the Judge asked you to wear a badge?"

"Too many to count."

"And you always say no."

"That's right."

"Why?"

"Haven't we talked about this before?" Clint asked.

"About why you don't wear a badge anymore," Reeves said. "But why do you keep turning down the Judge?"

"Oh, that's easy," Clint said. "I don't like him."

"Why not?"

"I'm not sure," Clint said. "Maybe it's because he

doesn't require proof before assuming one of his men is dead."

Washington and his men rode into Kilkenny just before dark. They stopped in front of the hotel. Washington gave his horse to Gordon, told them both to take care of the mounts.

"Both of us?" Franklin asked.

"Yeah, both of you."

They rode off toward the livery.

Washington went into the hotel. Jefferson was sitting in the lobby, waiting.

"Where are the others?" Washington asked.

"In their rooms, or in a whorehouse, one of the two," Jefferson said.

"Do I have a room?"

Jefferson nodded and handed him a key. Gordon and Franklin would get their own room when they came in.

"Are you sure Reeves will come?" Jefferson asked.

"I'm sure," Washington said. "Ain't you?"

"I think so," Jefferson said, "and I hope so, but—"

"Don't worry," Washington said, putting his hand on the other man's arm, "I'm sure."

TWENTY-SIX

Clint woke Reeves in the morning and said, "Let's go to Kilkenny for breakfast."

"Suits me," Reeves said.

They saddled up, and within two hours, they were riding into Kilkenny, Kansas. It was a small town, and Clint wondered what could possibly interest the Buffalo Soldier Bandits—as he had come to think of them—in this town.

"They got a bank," Reeves said as they rode past it.

"Kind of small, though."

Reeves nodded.

They rode a little farther and Reeves said, "Two hotels, two saloons."

"We'll pick one of each later," Clint said, "but maybe we should talk to the local law first."

"Right."

They found the sheriff's office and reined in.

"You better do the talking," Clint said as they dismounted. "You've got the badge."

"Yeah, you keep remindin' me," Reeves said. "You sure you don't want me to hide it?"

"No," Clint said, "I think it's important the sheriff sees it—oh, yeah, you were joking. You do it so rarely I didn't notice."

Reeves gave him a look, and they mounted the board-walk in front of the office.

Across the street a black man stood in the shadows, watched Clint and Reeves enter the sheriff's office. Then he came out of the shadows and hurried down the street.

Sergeant Lemuel Washington nursed his beer, sitting across from Corporal Jefferson. Three of the other four—Franklin, Weatherby, and Webster—were elsewhere. Their only instructions were to stay out of sight.

The batwings opened and Private Gordon entered, walking fast. He hurriedly joined Washington and Jefferson at the table.

"They're here," he said.

"Are you sure?" Jefferson asked.

"Yeah," Gordon said, "one of them was a great big black man."

"Reeves," Washington said.

"And the other man was white."

"Don't know who that is," Washington said, "but it don't matter. As long as Bass Reeves is here."

"So what are we gon' do now?" Jefferson asked.

After Private Edwards—who Washington was sure

was dead—Jefferson was the oldest of the men, and the sergeant often looked to him for advice.

"Gordon," Washington said, "get yourself a beer."

"Yessir. Don't got to tell me that twice."

"Then sit by yourself and drink it."

"Uh, okay, yessir."

"Now!" Washington said.

Gordon got up and walked to the bar.

"What are we gonna do now?" Washington asked. "I'm gonna talk to 'im."

"Talk to Bass Reeves?" Jefferson said. "You sure that's smart?"

"I want him to know," Washington said. "I want him to know it's me."

"But—"

"Ain't no buts, Corporal," Washington said. "That's part of all this, that Bass Reeves ends up knowin' it's me behind all this."

"Don't you think," Jefferson said, "we should find who's with him before we make a move?"

Washington frowned.

"You're probably right," he said, "but I can do that at the same time. After all, I'm just gonna talk to him first."

"When you gon' do that?"

"I guess," Washington said, "as soon as he cuts into a nice juicy steak."

TWENTY-SEVEN

"Sheriff Harry Riggs," the lawman said after Reeves introduced himself. "Glad ta meet you, Deputy. I heard a lot about you."

"This here's Clint Adams, he's ridin' with me," Reeves said.

Now Riggs's eyes really widened.

"The Gunsmith?" he said. "In my town?"

"We're trackin' some men," Reeves said. "The trail has led us here."

"Well, have a seat," Riggs said. He lowered his bulk into his chair. He wasn't fat, but he was so barrel-chested his chair creaked in protest.

Reeves and Clint remained standing.

"We're lookin' for black men," Reeves said. "Either three of 'em, or six."

"Three or six?"

"There's two groups, but they may have joined up," Reeves said.

"Well," Riggs said, "we got some black men in town, but I don't think you'd be trackin' them."

"Oh? Why not?"

"These here fellas is Buffalo Soldiers," Riggs said.

Clint and Reeves exchanged a glance, then looked back at the sheriff, who was sure that settled that . . .

Washington caught Gordon's eyes and waved him over. The man hurried to join them, carrying his beer.

"Finish that up," Washington said.

"Yessir!" Gordon thought his sergeant wanted him to finish so the man could buy him another beer.

"I want you to find the others," Washington said instead. "I want you to make sure that you, and they, stay out of sight until you hear from me, or from the corporal. Understand?"

"No, sir."

"Well, you don't have to understand," Jefferson said. "Just do it."

"Yessir. I'll take care of it."

"Then go!" Jefferson said.

"Sir!"

The man hurried out of the saloon.

"If they're talkin' to the sheriff, he's gon' tell him we're here, ya know."

"I know," Washington said. "I'm countin' on it."

Jefferson shook his head and drank some of his beer. Washington was just looking off into the distance.

* * *

"Buffalo Soldiers?" the sheriff said. "Robbing bank? Shootin' folks?"

"That's the way it looks," Reeves said.

"Well, I find that hard to believe," Riggs Said. "And if they was, what're they doin' out in the open here in Kilkenny?"

"We're in Kansas," Reeves said. "They been doin' all their dirty work in the Territories."

"You sure it's these fellers?" Riggs asked.

"That's what we're here to find out, Sheriff," Clint said.

"Well," Riggs said, looking distressed, "I'll do what I can to help you . . ."

"Do you have any deputies?"

"No," Riggs said, "we're a small town. There's just me."

"Have you spoken with these men?" Reeves asked.

"No."

"Why not?"

"I didn't see no reason to," Riggs said. "They're Buffalo Soldiers. I figured if they needed my help, they'd ask."

"Well," Clint said, "that would make sense if they were still Buffalo Soldiers."

"They're not?" Riggs asked. "They're wearin' the jackets."

Clint and Reeves remained silent and exchanged a look.

"What is it?" Riggs asked.

"Just a thought that we both had," Clint said. He looked at Reeves again, who nodded. "If these are the men we're looking for," Clint said, "we assumed they were no longer Buffalo Soldiers."

"But now you think . . ."

"If they are still Buffalo Soldiers," Reeves said, "then this is even worse than I thought."

"We should check," Clint said. "Do you have a telegraph in town?"

"No."

"We don't have any names," Reeves said. "We'll have to do it another way."

"How?" Riggs asked.

"We'll ask 'em."

TWENTY-EIGHT

"So where do we go now?" Jefferson asked.

"I go nowhere," Washington said. "I'll just wait here for Bass Reeves to find me."

"And what do I do?"

"I want you to keep an eye on the white man with Reeves," Washington said. "They'll probably come in here together. You let me do the talkin', and you just watch. If the white man makes a move, you kill him. Understand?"

"I understand."

"And go slow with the beer," the sergeant said. "Just nurse one. I don't want you drunk when they get here." Washington slapped Jefferson on the shoulder. "This is goin' the way we planned, Corporal."

Actually, Jefferson thought, this was going the way Washington had planned. Jefferson had just come along for the ride, like the others. For money, because they were tired of doing the white man's work for peanuts.

"Okay, Sarge," he said. "Okay."

*   *   *

Reeves and Clint left the sheriff's office, stopped just outside by their horses.

"How do you want to play this?" Clint asked.

Reeves thought a moment.

"If they rode into town bold as brass with their Buffalo Soldier jackets on, then they're expectin' us to find them."

"You think they're waiting for us?"

Reeves nodded.

"Then they're probably in one of the saloons," Clint said.

"Probably."

"Which one you want to try first?"

"None," Reeves said. "Let's make them wait for us. We'll take care of the horses, get our hotel rooms, and something to eat. Then we'll go and find them."

"Unless they find us first."

"They might do that," Reeves said, "but back when three of them ambushed us, they all could've done it. They probably could've killed us then."

"But they didn't want to."

"No," Reeves said. "They wanna talk to us."

"To you," Clint said. "They want to talk to you. They probably don't even know who I am."

"You're right," Reeves said. "That's good. We won't tell them who you are until we have to."

"That'll be our ace in the hole."

"Right."

"So, the livery first?"

"Yeah," Reeves said. "Let's go."

They walked their mounts to the livery.

As in most places, the liveryman was impressed with Eclipse, but this particular man did not connect the horse to the Gunsmith, which pleased them.

"How long you gonna want to leave these horses here, Deputy?"

"We're not sure," Reeves said. "One or two days."

"Okay. I got room."

They were about to leave with their rifles and saddle-bags when Reeves turned back to the man.

"Did the Buffalo Soldiers leave their horses here?" he asked.

"Yessir," the man said. "I got them out back on the corral."

"How many?"

"Six."

Reeves looked at Clint.

"Six," he said.

"Six." Clint nodded.

They headed for the hotel.

They got a room each, again across from each other. Clint left his gear in his room and joined Reeves across the hall. The big black man was looking out the window at the street below.

"Anybody?" Clint asked.

"No," Reeves said. "We're not bein' watched now."

Reeves turned from the window.

"I'm startin' to get a bad feelin'," he said.

"Tell me," Clint said. "Maybe it's the same bad feeling I'm getting."

"That we been led here by the nose?" Reeves asked.

"That's the one," Clint said, "or else why would they have stopped here?"

"And not even put a watch on us."

Reeves went back to the window.

"Six of 'em," he said, "and what are they doin' if they're not watchin' us?"

"What do most men do when they hit a town?" Clint asked. "Eat, drink, or fuck."

Reeves looked at Clint.

"Let's eat and drink," he said.

"Agreed," Clint said.

TWENTY-NINE

Clint and Reeves went out and found a place where they could get a beer and a steak. They got a table away from the window and ordered.

"Six men waiting for us," Clint said, "and they're apparently not waiting to ambush us."

"They wanted me to follow them," Reeves said, "out of the Territories."

"They wanted to get you out of your jurisdiction," Clint said, "and alone."

"But why?" Reeves asked. "Why me?"

"Well . . . you're famous."

"I ain't goddamned famous," Reeves said. "You're famous."

"Well, you're a well-known black lawman," Clint said, "and these are black men."

"Black men," Reeves said. "Also black lawmen. What do they have against me?"

"I guess that's something we're going to have to ask them," Clint said.

"Take a walk," Washington told Jefferson.

"What?"

"Take a walk around town, see what you can see," the sergeant said.

"What if they see me?"

"If they do, and they stop you, bring them here," Washington said. "Tell them I'm here."

"What if they just . . . kill me on sight?" Jefferson asked.

Washington smiled.

"I know Bass Reeves well enough to know he won't do that," Washington said.

"What about sending Gordon? Or—"

"I don't care who you send, just have someone take a look around town. I want to know where they are, what they're doin'."

"Okay," Jefferson said, "I can do that."

He stood up.

"Also check the hotels," Washington said. "I want to know where they are—and who the white man is. We need to know what we're dealin' with."

"Yessir." Jefferson seemed calmer now that he didn't necessarily have to be the one looking for Reeves and his partner.

He left the saloon and went in search of the others.

Washington went to the bar to get himself another beer.

"You fellas ain't lookin' for trouble in town, are ya?" the bartender asked.

"Why do you ask that?" Washington asked.

"Well," the bartender said, "half a dozen Buffalo Soldiers hangin' around town, folks start to talk. Ya know . . ."

"Well," Washington said, "you tell folks not to worry. We ain't lookin' for trouble."

"That's good—"

"But know this," Washington added, "if it happens to come along, we'll take care of it. Don't you worry about that."

He carried his fresh beer back to the table and sat down.

The bartender started cleaning the bar with a dirty rag, not feeling any better for the short conversation.

Jefferson found both Franklin and Gordon at the local cathouse.

He broke in on Franklin while he was pounding away at a fat whore. The skinny black man loved his women with meat on them, always asked for the biggest whore he could get. This one had massive thighs, pale as the moon, and they jiggled as Franklin drove himself in and out of her, grunting with the effort.

"Ten-hut!" Jefferson shouted.

Franklin leaped off the woman to spring to attention, his long, skinny dick sticking straight out from his crotch, glistening with the girl's juices. Jefferson averted his eyes.

When he saw Jefferson, he said, "Aw, goddamn, Corporal, you scared the crap outta me."

"Sorry, Private, but we got some work for you," Jefferson said with a wide grin.

The woman sat up. Her breasts were huge mounds of pale flesh with the biggest pink nipples he'd ever seen before. The hair on her head was as golden as the hair between her legs.

"Get dressed," Jefferson said. "I've gotta find Gordon."

"Probably down the hall," Franklin said.

"I'll check."

The woman looked at Jefferson and smiled. Despite the weight in her face, she was very pretty.

"You sure you don't wanna finish what your friend started, honey?" she asked with a smile. "I'm all warmed up for ya."

"Thank you, ma'am," Jefferson said politely. "Maybe another time."

He left them and went down the hall, opened the door. Gordon had not even had time to get his pants off yet. A dark-haired, skinny whore was waiting on the bed for him, fully naked.

"Aw, Corporal—" he said when he saw Jefferson. "Come on!"

"Sorry," Jefferson said. "Get your pants back on and meet me downstairs."

"Yes, sir."

As Jefferson left, he heard the whore say, "I still get paid, right?"

THIRTY

He waited outside for his two men, who came out to join him glumly. He told them both what he wanted them to do.

"What if they see me?" Franklin asked.

"Don't worry," Jefferson said, "they gon' wanna talk to the man in charge. You jes' take 'em over to the saloon."

"Where you gon' be when I find out what hotel they's in?" Gordon asked.

"I'll be at the saloon, with the sergeant," Jefferson said. "You jes' come over there and tell us."

The two men shrugged and went their separate ways. Jefferson stood there, waited until they were out of sight, then went back inside. After all, Washington had told him to stay out of sight.

He hoped the fat whore hadn't got dressed again yet.

Franklin finally spotted Bass Reeves and the white man in a restaurant eating steaks. He watched them for a moment, trying to get some idea how long they'd be there, then turned and headed for the saloon. He ran into Gordon on the way, who was also hurrying.

"You find 'em?" he asked.

"Yeah, they's eatin' steaks. You find out who that white man is?"

"Man," Gordon said, "you ain't gon' believes me when I tell you."

"Well, go ahead, then."

"We might's well wait 'til we get to the saloon," Gordon said. "I'll tell the sergeant and Jefferson at the same time."

Jefferson had time to dally with the fat whore and get back to the saloon before Franklin and Gordon got there. He was sitting with Washington, having a beer.

"You boys get it done?" the corporal asked.

"Yeah, we did," Franklin said. "They's at a café having steaks, but Gordon here, he say he got some big news fo' us."

Washington looked at Gordon.

"Whataya got for us, Private?"

"They registered at the Main Street Hotel, sir," Gordon said. "They got themselves rooms of they own."

"And what's the big news, Corporal?" Washington asked.

"Well, sir," Gordon said, "the name of that white man that's ridin' with Bass Reeves?"

"Yes, Corporal?"

"Well, sir," Gordon said, "his name is Clint Adams."

They all sat silently.

"He's the Gunsmith," Gordon said.

"I know who he is!" Washington said.

"Why would Reeves have the Gunsmith ridin' with him?" Jefferson asked.

"Maybe they're friends," Washington said. "Why would a white man ride all this way with a black man if they wasn't friends?"

"Could be," Jefferson said.

Gordon and Franklin stood there, waiting for their next set of orders.

"You two are done," Washington said with a wave of his hand. "Go get a drink, or a woman, or whatever you wanna do."

"Yessir," Franklin said.

He left and went straight back to the whorehouse. Gordon stopped at the bar for a beer, and remained there.

Jefferson sat back in his chair and watched Washington. The sergeant was lost in his thoughts. Jefferson sipped his beer and waited, but finally felt he had to ask something.

"So what do we do now?"

"Hmm?" Washington looked at him. "Oh, nothin' gonna change."

"With the Gunsmith here?"

"He don't scare me none," Washington said.

"Well, he scares me," Jefferson said. "He gon' scare the others."

"Then it's best that I'm the leader, right?" Washington asked.

Jefferson nodded. In all the time he'd been riding with

Washington, never was he more grateful that the sergeant was the leader, and not him.

"Get a couple of more beers, will ya, Corporal?" Washington said. "I gotta sit here and figure out what to do about the Gunsmith."

THIRTY-ONE

Clint and Reeves finished their steaks, had some more coffee with pie.

"Well?" Clint asked.

"Yeah," Reeves said. "We better go and find them boys."

"We're just going to talk at first, right?" Clint asked.

"Yeah, right," Reeves said, "we ain't gonna try to take 'em until after we talk to 'em. Unless they start shootin' first."

"I know you want to talk to these boys, find out what's on their mind, but if I get shot at," Clint said, "I'm going to shoot back."

"Understood," Reeves said.

They had the last bite of their pie, and the last sip of coffee, then paid their bill and walked out of the restaurant. There was a saloon right across the street.

"Let's try that one first," Reeves said.

* * *

When they walked in, Bass Reeves was the only black man in the saloon.

"Let's get a drink," he said.

"Sure," Clint said.

They went to the bar, ordered a beer each.

"Here ya go," the bartender said. "You with them other fellers?"

"What other fellas?" Reeves asked.

"Them other black boys that rode in," the bartender said. "The ones wearin' them jackets."

"Buffalo Soldier jackets, you mean?" Reeves asked.

The bartender, a young man in his twenties, said, "I don't know. They're blue, and they got stripes on their arms."

"How many stripes?" Clint asked.

"Mostly one," the young man said. "I think one of 'em's got two and another one's got three."

"Did they drink in here?" Clint asked.

"A few of them had a drink in here," the bartender said, "but the others are drinkin' down the street, in the Wagon Wheel."

"When did they arrive?" Reeves asked. It was a question he'd forgotten to ask the sheriff.

"Yesterday," the bartender said. "They only been here a day."

Reeves nodded. He looked around, saw that he was the center of attention.

"Don't have too many black folk in this town, do ya?" he asked.

"None," the bartender said, "until they rode in yesterday, and now you."

"Well," Reeves said, "maybe by tomorrow you'll be back to havin' none."

"That suits us!" someone spoke up.

Clint and Reeves turned. The man who had spoken was easily identified.

"You got something to say?" Clint asked.

"Yeah," the man said, standing. He was tall, in his forties, wearing a well-worn gun on his hip. "We don't need all you black boys here, lawmen or not."

"Then why don't you drive them out?" Reeves asked.

The man looked around, licked his lips, and looked like he was sorry he'd spoken.

"I—I can't do it myself," he said.

"And nobody will stand with you?" Clint asked, looking at the other men in the saloon.

They all looked away.

"No," the man said, "nobody."

"Well," Reeves said, "you could stand alone against me." He stepped away from the bar. "Drive me out of your town."

The man put his hands out in front of him, away from his gun.

"Easy now, Deputy," he said. "I ain't lookin' for trouble."

"Then shut your mouth," Reeves said. "Sit down and don't say nothin' else."

"Okay," the man said, "okay." He sat down.

Clint kept an eye on the man, just in case he got brave and went for his gun.

"Bass," Clint said, "let's get out of here."

They backed to the batwing door and went outside.

"We need to get this done before somebody else gets brave," Clint said.

"You're right," Reeves said. "We better get over to the Wagon Wheel Saloon."

"He said down the street," Clint said. "But which way?"

Reeves looked both ways, then shrugged and said, "We'll try both."

THIRTY-TWO

Gordon was standing at the batwings. He turned and hurried to Washington's table.

"They're coming down the street."

"Okay," Washington said. "Stand at the bar, and no matter what happens, don't go for your gun."

"Yessir."

"What about me?" Jefferson asked.

"Stay where you are," Washington said. "Bass will know you."

"Yeah, he will."

"This will shake him up," Washington said. "Disappoint him."

"What do you think he'll do?"

"Bass?" Washington laughed. "He'll wanna know why. He'll talk before he does anythin'."

"I hope you're right."

"You just sit tight," Washington said. "Don't talk. Just listen."

                    *   *   *

Clint and Reeves approached the Wagon Wheel Saloon.
From the outside it looked larger than the place they'd
just left.

"See that man at the doors?" Clint asked.

"I saw him."

"They know we're coming."

"This is what they wanted," Reeves said. "This is what
they're gonna get."

"You want me to go around back?" Clint asked.

"No," Reeves said, "they know about you. If they
planned this, they already checked the hotel register.
They know who you are."

"You're probably right."

"We'll just walk in together and let them call the play,"
Reeves said.

Clint nodded. They mounted the boardwalk and went
through the batwings.

What Bass Reeves saw froze him in his tracks. Clint
knew something was up.

"What is it?"

Reeves didn't answer.

There was one Buffalo Soldier standing at the bar, and
two seated at a table. The two at the table had corporal's
and sergeant's stripes, while the one at the bar had a
single private's stripe.

But Bass Reeves was looking at the men at the table.
Clint didn't know which one, but he could guess. The
younger one, with the three stripes, was smiling at the
big black lawman.

"Bass," the man said. "Finally."

"Can't be," Reeves said. "You're dead."

"I am?" the sergeant said. "I feel pretty good for somebody who's dead."

Reeves looked at the other man.

"Jefferson."

"Bass."

"You fellas have come a long way," Reeves said.

Jefferson laughed. "Ain't we all?"

Reeves looked at the man at the bar. "I don't know you."

The man didn't answer.

"And you're the Gunsmith," the sergeant said. "My name's Lemuel Washington, sergeant in the Buffalo Soldiers. This is Corporal Jefferson, and that's Private Gordon."

"Should be three more of you around here someplace," Clint said.

"Oh, yeah," Washington said. "They're whorin' or drinkin'—or both. But they'll be here when I need them."

"Okay," Clint said, "so you know these two."

"Yes," Reeves said, "years ago. I thought Washington was dead."

"You've come a long way, Bass," Washington said. "Wearin' a badge for Judge Parker."

"And you, Lem?" Reeves asked. "What are you doin'? Are you still a Buffalo Soldier, or are you and your boys just wearin' the jackets?"

"Well, Bass," Washington said, "it wouldn't be right for us to wear these jackets if we wasn't still Buffalo Soldiers, would we?"

"It ain't right for you to be robbin' and killin' people while you're still with the Soldiers, Lem," Reeves shot back.

"I got an idea, Bass," Washington said. "Sit down with us and have a beer. You and your friend. We got lots to talk about. Lots of catchin' up to do."

Reeves looked at Clint, who shrugged and said, "Why not? We said we'd let them call the play. Looks like their play is drinking."

"Gordon," Washington said, "four beers."

THIRTY-THREE

Reeves and Clint sat with Washington and Jefferson. Gordon came over with four mugs of beer.

"Back to the bar, Private," Washington said.

"Yessir."

There were others in the place, but by the time Gordon returned to his place at the bar, they had all cleared out. All that was left was the bartender.

"What's this all about, Lem?" Bass Reeves asked. "You can't expect the Buffalo Soldiers to take you back after what you've all done."

"Well," Washington said, "nobody knows we done it except for you and Adams here. So all we gotta do is make sure you don't tell nobody."

"How do you expect to do that?"

"Well . . . we could kill you," Washington said.

"That's why you led me here?" Reeves asked. "To kill me? Is that why you did all of this? To get me to hunt you?"

"Not to hunt us," Washington said. "To find us, which you did. You're good at yer job, Bass. I was countin' on that."

Reeves sat back and regarded the man. Clint wondered what the relationship was between them. It was something he'd have to ask Reeves later, when they were alone.

"So what do we do now, Lem?" Reeves asked.

Washington shrugged.

"You do what you gotta do, Bass," he said. "Me and my boys are here, we ain't goin' anywhere."

"So you're darin' me to take you in?"

"Oh yeah," Washington said, smiling with teeth that were more yellow than white. "That's what I'm doin'. I dare ya to take us in."

"What if I decide just to take you in, Lem?" Reeves asked. "What if I forget about your boys, let 'em go. Clint and me, we just take you."

"My boys ain't gonna just sit by and let you take me, Bass," Washington said. "See, we're in this together."

"In what together?" Reeves asked, "Just what the hell is it you think you're doin'?"

"I'm gettin' what's comin' to me," Washington said. "We're all gettin' what's comin' to us." The sergeant leaned forward in his chair. "And so are you." He looked at Clint. "You're just in the way, Adams. Wrong place, wrong time. I was you, I'd ride out. This is between me and Bass."

"I'm not about to let Bass face six men alone, Washington," Clint said, "so you can forget that. I don't know what's going on between you two, but I came all this way with Bass and I'm staying."

"Suit yourself," Washington said.

"Why don't we take you right now?" Reeves asked. "There's only three of you."

"Whatever you say, Bass," Washington said, spreading his arms. "You call the play."

Clint eased away from the table a bit, just in case Reeves did just that.

The black deputy picked up his beer and drained the half that was left.

Clint drank his as well. He felt they were about to leave.

"No, not yet," Reeves said, standing.

Clint was surprised at how relaxed Sergeant Lem Washington appeared to be. He apparently had no doubt that Reeves was leaving, and that the lawman wouldn't change his mind and go for his gun.

"We'll be seein' you later, Lem," Reeves said.

"I ain't leavin' town, Bass," Washington said. "None of us is. You don't know my other men, but they're good boys. They're ready."

"Good," Reeves said. "They'll need to be."

He backed to the door with Clint alongside him, then turned and walked out. Clint gave Washington one last look, took a last glance at the man at the bar, then backed out the doors.

Outside Bass Reeves was standing still, hands on his hips. People walking on the boardwalk gave him a wide berth.

"That was interesting," Clint said.

Reeves looked at him.

"You're probably confused."

"I'm . . . puzzled."

"Let's go someplace," Reeves said. "I got some things ta tell ya."

"That was fun," Washington said.

"Fun?" Jefferson's muscles were still tense. He'd kept waiting for Bass Reeves or the Gunsmith to go for their gun. "Jesus."

"Don't worry, Corporal," Washington said. "Everything's goin' the way I planned."

THIRTY-FOUR

They walked up the street to the other, smaller saloon and took beers to a back table. Some of the patrons had moved over from the Wagon Wheel, and now that they saw Clint and Bass Reeves, they shook their heads and left to go back there.

"I've known Lem Washington a long time," Bass Reeves said.

"I figured that much."

"We joined at the same time, went to the Academy together, where Jefferson was an instructor," Clint said.

"So the three of you were friends?"

"For a short time."

"What happened?"

"What usually happens?"

"A woman?"

Reeves nodded.

"I don't wanna go over the whole thing, but she picked me over him . . . and then she died," Reeves said. "Lem blamed me."

"And Jefferson?"

"He sided with Lem."

"So because you and he had a problem over a woman, he turns from being a Buffalo Soldier lawman to a killer? And takes five men with him?" Clint shook his head. "I don't buy it. There's something else going on."

"Like what?"

"I don't know," Clint said. "If I did, I wouldn't be puzzled."

"Well," Reeves said, "whatever the reason is, I gotta take him and the others in."

"Fine," Clint said, "when do you want to do it?"

"I guess we shoulda done it in the saloon," Reeves said.

"We could have," Clint said. "We'd have three of them already, but what the hell. We might as well take all six of them."

"At one time?" Reeves asked.

"Why not?" Clint said. "We'd have them right where we want them, wouldn't we?"

"Lem Washington's a good man, Clint," Reeves said. "So is Jefferson. We don't know about the others, but if Lem says they're good boys, I'd believe 'im."

"Then maybe we ought to find out who they are, and where they are."

"That's a good idea . . ."

* * *

They left the small saloon and walked over to the sheriff's office. The lawman was seated behind his desk, looked up at them in surprise.

"Back again? Need help?"

"We need to know where the other three Buffalo Soldiers are," Reeves said.

"They ain't in the Wagon Wheel?"

"Three of them are," Clint said. "We need to know where the other three are."

"Or might be."

"You check the other saloon?"

"Just came from there," Clint said.

"Hmm . . ." the lawman said, giving the question some thought.

"Where's the whorehouse?" Reeves asked.

"You think they'd go there?" the sheriff asked. "Ain't no black whores that I know of."

Clint stared at the man. Did he really think black men only went with black whores?

"That's okay," he said. "I don't think they'll mind, as long as there's women."

"Oh, well, there's women," Riggs said.

"Good," Clint said. "Just tell us where the whorehouse is, and we'll take care of the rest."

When Clint and Reeves walked into the whorehouse, the madam confronted them, looking the black lawman up and down.

"Well," she said, "it seems to be our week for black men, but you're somethin' special."

"I'm a deputy marshal," Reeves said.

"And a great big man," the fiftyish madam said. "Makes me wish I was younger. Hey, girls, look what I got for you!"

The girls came out into the hall from the parlor, and most of them were as impressed with Bass Reeves as the madam was.

They crowded around the big man, touching him, rubbing his arms and his broad chest. He looked over at Clint, as if pleading for help, but all Clint could do was shrug and stay out of the way.

"Do you have other black men here?" Reeves asked the madam.

"Oh, are you with them?" she asked.

"I'm lookin' for them," Reeves said, still being touched by the eager whores. He finally decided to address them. "Ladies, I'm here on official business."

"I got some official business for you, honey," a red-haired whore said. "Right here." She pulled open her robe to show her naked body beneath it. She had pale, small breasts with dusky nipples and a spray of freckles.

"All right, ladies," Clint said, "I think you should all go back into the parlor. The deputy has some business to tend to."

"What about you, handsome?" the redhead asked. "You got business?"

"I guess I do. Sorry. Come on, ladies."

Clint herded all the sweet-smelling women back into the parlor.

"Ma'am," Reeves said, "how many of them are here?"

"There's two of 'em upstairs," she said. "The other one left about an hour ago."

"Did he say where he was goin'?"

"That's not part of the deal," she said. "Men come here for pussy, and when they leave, they don't tell me where they're goin'. Are you interested in a girl, Deputy?"

"Not right now."

"Well then," she said, "the two men you're interested in are upstairs in rooms two and five. I got work to do."

She turned and left the hall, passing Clint on the way.

"We going upstairs?" Clint asked.

"I don't want them to panic," Reeves said. "One of the girls might get hurt. Why don't we wait for them to come outside?"

"Good," Clint said, "then we can take them outside."

"Well, before we try to take 'em," Reeves said, "I'd like to talk to 'em. Maybe we can get them to turn themselves in. Or maybe we can convince them not to follow Washington."

"Bass, if you want to try talking to them first, I'll back you. If you want to try and take them, I'll back you there, too."

"I know you will, Clint," Reeves said. "I appreciate everythin' you've done for me so far, and I'm sorry this turned out to be so personal."

Clint looked into the parlor and said, "I think we better take this outside before you get mobbed by a bunch of hungry whores again, Bass."

The black lawman didn't argue.

THIRTY-FIVE

Washington waved Gordon over from the bar.

"Yessir?"

"You know where the others are?"

"Last I saw, they was at the whorehouse."

"Well, you go and get them outta that whorehouse before they wear off their tallywackers," Jefferson said. "We all gotta be ready for when Reeves and Adams come fer us."

"Sir?" Gordon looked at Washington.

"I want all three of them here in one hour," Washington said. "You, too. Weapons ready."

"Yessir."

Gordon went back to the bar to finish his beer.

"Leave that!" Washington said. "Just go!"

"Yessir."

After he was gone, Jefferson asked, "Do you think they'll still follow when they find out it's personal between you and Bass?"

"They better," Washington said, "or they'll have to face me."

The whorehouse was a two-story building that used to be a boardinghouse until the madam took it over. There were five steps up to a porch and the front door. Reeves and Clint took up position on the porch to wait.

When Gordon reached the whorehouse, he saw the two men on the porch, and recognized them. He turned and ran back to the saloon.

Washington was surprised when he saw Gordon come back into the saloon.

"That fast?"

"I went to the whorehouse, sir," Gordon said. "The deputy and Clint Adams are on the porch."

"Doin' what?"

"They look like they's just waitin'."

Washington looked at Jefferson.

"They gonna take our boys out first?" Jefferson asked.

"No," Washington said, "that ain't the way Bass does things."

"No? What about Adams?"

"Bass is the one wearin' the badge," Washington said. "Adams will go along with what he says."

"And what's he gonna say?"

"He'll tell Adams that he wants to take us all together."

"That's crazy."

"Bass Reeves and Clint Adams? Why would they be afraid to face six men? They's legends."

"Six Buffalo Soldiers," Jefferson said. "With special trainin'."

"Men like them got egos," Washington said. "They'll face all of us, and then they'll die."

He looked at Gordon.

"You just march into that whorehouse right past them."

"W-What if they stop me?"

"They won't."

"What if they kill me?"

"They won't," Washington insisted.

"Sir—"

"You have your orders, Private."

"Yessir."

Gordon left.

"This woulda been easier," Jefferson said, "with nine men."

Washington pointed a finger at his corporal and said, "Don't start."

THIRTY-SIX

"Here he comes again," Clint said.

Reeves and Clint had both seen Private Gordon earlier, before he'd turned and run back to the saloon. Now they saw him coming back, walking very slowly.

"Washington told him to walk in, right past us," Reeves said.

"He looks scared."

"He thinks we might stop him, or worse, kill him," Reeves said.

"But we're going to let him go in."

"Right."

"Bass—"

"These are Buffalo Soldiers, Clint," Reeves said as the black private approached. "They deserve to be taken in head on, all together. No tricks."

Gordon reached the steps, mounted them slowly, and

walked past them with his shoulders hunched. He entered the house and closed the door behind him.

"Okay," Clint said, "no tricks."

Gordon was not besieged by whores the way Reeves had been. He was not the physical specimen that Bass Reeves was, so the girls in the parlor ignored him.

He told the madam he was looking for his friends, and she told him the same thing she had told Reeves, rooms two and five. Gordon nodded and went upstairs.

He didn't want to see his friends naked, so he knocked on the doors, then opened them slightly and said the same thing.

"Time to go. The sarge wants us in the saloon in an hour."

"Then I still got time," Franklin said. "Go away."

"I'll be there!" Carl Weatherby snapped. "Go away."

"Where's Webster?" Gordon asked them both.

He got the same answer.

"Who knows?"

He closed the doors and went back downstairs, nervous about the fact that he still had to go out past Reeves and Adams.

Should he have warned Weatherby and Franklin?

Naw, let 'em find out for themselves.

When Gordon came back out, he looked nervously at Reeves and Clint. Reeves gave him a stony, silent glare, while Clint actually smiled at him.

"Think we should have asked him when the others were coming out?" Clint asked.

"Naw," Reeves said. "He delivered a message to them. Lem probably wants them in the saloon. They'll be comin' out."

"Hope they don't panic and go for their guns when they see us."

"Washington said they were good boys," Reeves said. "I don't think they'll do anythin' stupid."

As far as Clint was concerned, everything these men had done—especially following Lem Washington—had been stupid, but he held his tongue.

A half an hour later the door opened and two black men came out, hitching up their trousers and holsters. They froze when they saw Clint and Bass Reeves.

THIRTY-SEVEN

"Hello, boys," Reeves said.

Neither man spoke, or moved. Clint could tell from Reeves's reaction that he did not know either of the two men. However, the two men knew who Bass Reeves was on sight. Either that, or Gordon had warned them. If that was the case, they also knew who Clint was, but he didn't get that feeling.

So he just stood there silently, while they stared at Reeves and the badge on his chest.

"You boys know who I am, right?"

Both men, appearing to be in their thirties, nodded.

"I had a talk with your boss," Reeves said. "He's an old friend of mine, did you know that?"

"No," Weatherby said, "we didn't."

"Yeah," Reeves said, "I think this whole thing might be gettin' kinda personal. You men oughta think about that. You wanna go to jail, or worse, die because of a personal grudge?"

The men didn't respond.

"Yeah, well," Reeves said, "you oughta talk to your sergeant about that."

Neither man moved.

"That's okay," Reeves told them. "You can go. I just wanted you to know that."

The two men went down the steps and headed toward town, but Reeves stepped forward and said, "Hey!"

They turned quickly, crouched, then straightened when they saw he hadn't drawn his gun.

"What are your last names?" Reeves asked.

They looked at each other, and then one of them said, "I'm Franklin, he's Weatherby."

"We already talked to Washington and Jefferson, and their other man, Gordon. There's a sixth man. What's his name?"

Again the men exchanged a look, then Franklin said, "That's Private Webster."

"Webster," Reeves said. "And where's he now?"

"We don't know," Franklin said.

"He was here," Weatherby said, "but we don't know where he is now."

"Okay," Reeves said. "Go. We'll be seeing you later. And by 'we,' I mean me and my friend here, Clint Adams."

Clint could see that his name registered with them just before they turned and trotted off.

Reeves looked at Clint and said, "Sorry. I just wanted them to know . . ."

"Yeah, I know," Clint said. "That's okay."

They walked down the steps.

"So they're all going to be in that saloon," Clint said.

"We hope," Reeves said. "They have to find their sixth man."

"When do you want to take them?" Clint asked. "Five would be better than six. I mean, for us."

"We'd still have to hunt down the sixth man," Reeves said. "It's better to take them all at once."

"And you're sure we can do that," Clint said.

"Hey, you're the Gunsmith," Reeves said, "and I'm one of Judge Parker's deputies."

"And they are six well-trained Buffalo Soldiers," Clint reminded him. "I'm going along with this because it's your game, Bass, but somehow I think divide and conquer may have been a good idea."

"Remember what I said about tricks?"

"I remember," Clint said. "I'm just starting to think that maybe you weren't right."

"Now's not the time to argue," Reeves said.

"You're right," Clint said. "That time has passed."

Gordon found Webster sitting in front of a dress shop, talking to some kids—boys and girls, all white, from ages three to about ten.

"What are you doin'?" he asked.

"I'm just tellin' these kids some stories," Webster said. "They like my stories."

"We gotta go," Gordon said. "The sarge wants us at the saloon."

"But we want more stories," a ten-year-old boy said.

"Hey," Webster said to the boy, "duty calls. You remember what I tol' you about duty?"

"Yessir," the boy said.

Webster stood up.

"I'll be back," he said. "You kids be good."

He walked with Gordon down the street.

"Instead of at the whorehouse, I find you with a bunch of kids?" Gordon asked.

"I like kids," Webster said. "What's goin' on?"

"It's time," Gordon said. "Bass Reeves is here, and he's got the Gunsmith with him."

"What? The white man is the Gunsmith?"

"Yup," Gordon said. "I hope you tol' them kids all the stories you got. You might not get a chance to tell them no more."

THIRTY-EIGHT

Washington and Jefferson looked up as Gordon and Webster entered the saloon. Against the bar were Weatherby and Franklin. There was no one else in the saloon except for the bartender.

"Get a beer, Private," Washington said to Webster.

"Yessir."

Webster went to the bar to join his partners. Gordon walked over to the table where Washington and Jefferson were sitting.

"Where was he?" Washington asked.

"He was, uh, talkin' to some kids, sir."

"Kids?"

"Tellin' them stories."

"Stories?"

"He was a teacher before he joined the Buffalo Soldiers," Jefferson said. "He likes kids."

"That's what he said, sir," Gordon said. "He likes kids."

"All right," Washington said. "Go and get a beer with the others."

"Yessir."

As Gordon walked away, Washington looked at Jefferson and said, "A teacher?"

"And he's a damned good soldier," Jefferson added. "They're all good boys."

"They better be," Washington said. He pushed his chair back.

"What now?"

"Now I tell them what we're up against," Washington said.

"Are you gonna tell 'em everythin'?"

Washington was in the act of standing. He paused and looked at his corporal.

"What do you mean by everythin'?" he asked.

"You know," Jefferson said. "You and Bass."

"I'll tell them that we know each other," Washington said, "and that when the time comes, Bass is mine. The rest of you will kill the Gunsmith."

"But what about—"

"Then you'll all have the reputation as the men who killed a legend," Washington said.

Jefferson stared at his commanding officer.

"Don't worry, Corporal," Washington said, "it's all gonna work out. Trust me."

Bass Reeves and Clint went to see Sheriff Riggs.

"How's everythin' goin'?" Riggs asked.

"It looks like we're gonna have to take these six men by force, Sheriff," Reeves said.

"And you want my help?"

"Not exactly," Clint said. "We only need you to know what's going to happen. We didn't want you to be surprised when you heard the shooting."

"Well, that's good," Riggs said, "because to tell you the truth, I wouldn't know which side to take. I mean, Buffalo Soldiers are law officers, right? And you're a deputy marshal. You gotta admit this is kind of an odd situation."

"We're fairly sure they're not Buffalo Soldiers anymore," Clint said. "Not after committing the robberies they have, and the killings."

"Well, yeah, but I don't know that for sure."

"That's why we're not askin' you to take sides, Sheriff," Reeves said. "Just . . . stay out of the way."

Riggs sat back in his chair and said, "I can do that."

Washington told his men that within the next day they would be facing both Bass Reeves and Clint Adams. Of course, they knew that Adams was the Gunsmith.

"We didn't know we would have to face him," Franklin said.

"I didn't either," Washington said. "I only expected Bass Reeves to track us. And maybe another deputy. The Gunsmith is a surprise."

"What can we do?" Weatherby asked.

"Kill him."

"Kill the Gunsmith?" Gordon asked.

"We'll need more men," Franklin said. "What about the others?"

"I believe that Reeves and the Gunsmith have already killed Private Edwards and the others."

"Then we have to run," Gordon said.

"No," Washington said. "I can kill Bass Reeves. That leaves the five of you to kill Clint Adams."

The four men standing at the bar exchanged glances with each other.

"Don't you think five trained Buffalo Soldiers can kill one man?" Washington asked. "Even if that one man is the Gunsmith?"

THIRTY-NINE

When they stepped outside the sheriff's office, they noticed how desolate the streets were.

"Word got around," Clint said.

"At least we won't have to worry about innocent bystanders," Reeves said.

"You really think those six men are going to face us in the street, fair and square?" Clint asked.

Reeves hesitated a moment, then said, "No. I'd expect that from Buffalo Soldiers, but not from these men. They'll try something underhanded. And we have to be ready."

Clint looked at Reeves and raised his eyebrows.

"What are you thinkin'?" Reeves asked.

"I'm thinking why should we be the ones waiting for them to make a move?" Clint said. "Let's make them think we're planning something of our own."

"Good idea," Reeves said. "If we make them wait, maybe they'll get impatient and make a mistake."

"How long?" Clint asked.

"I ain't in a hurry," Reeves said, "since we know where they all are."

"Five of them anyway."

"I'm sure Washington got ahold of his sixth man," Reeves said. "Believe me, they're all in the saloon."

"I saw a couple of wooden chairs in front of our hotel," Clint said. "Why don't we go and put them to good use?"

"Good idea."

"Where are they?" Jefferson asked.

"Don't get impatient," Washington said. "Bass Reeves is a smart man. He wants to keep us waitin' so we get nervous."

Jefferson looked over at the four fidgety black men standing at the bar. "I think it's workin'."

"Then go and talk to them," Washington said. "Calm them down."

"Okay."

Jefferson started to get up.

"But in the meantime," Washington added, "send Gordon out to see where they are."

"Yes sir."

Gordon griped at always being the one sent out to check on Reeves and Adams. He was sure that at some point they'd get tired of seeing him and just kill him.

He walked around town, finally saw the two men sitting on chairs in front of their hotel. He ducked into a doorway and just watched them for a few minutes, but they weren't doing anything but sitting.

He quit the doorway and moved away from the area, feeling safe that he hadn't been seen.

"See 'im?" Reeves asked.

"I see him."

"All right," Reeves said, "so now they know where we are."

"But Washington's a smart man, isn't he?" Clint asked.

"I used to think so."

"So maybe he's figurin' what we're doin'," Clint said. "He won't panic."

"Probably not," Reeves said, "but his men might."

"I'm getting hungry," Clint said.

"A hot meal sounds good," Reeves said. "We might as well eat early—we don't want to put a café full of people in danger."

They got up and went to find a nice empty restaurant.

Gordon came hurrying into the saloon.

"They're in front of their hotel," he told Washington and Jefferson.

"Doin' what?" Jefferson asked.

"Nothin'," Gordon said. "Just sittin' and talkin'."

"Did they see you?" Jefferson asked.

"I don't think so."

"Okay," Washington said. "Go back to the bar with the others."

Gordon did so gladly.

"They saw him," Washington said.

"Yeah," Jefferson said. "So what do we do?"

"We do what they're doin'," Washington said. "We make them wait."

"So we're all just waitin'?" the corporal asked.

"That's right."

"What about eatin'?"

"Eat whenever you want," Washington said, "as long as it's right here."

FORTY

Clint and Reeves found a small café with only about half a dozen tables. And while one was taken when they got there, the man and woman seated there got up and left as soon as it became clear they were going to stay and eat.

"Oh yeah," Clint said, "word has gotten around there's going to be trouble."

The waiter nervously told them to take any table. They sat as far from the window as they could, just in case.

They ordered steaks, and while they were a little tough, they weren't as tough as the beef jerky they'd been dining on. They each washed the food down with a mug of beer.

They were on to coffee and pie when Sheriff Riggs walked into the place. The café was still empty, so he walked right over to them.

"You found my place," Riggs said.

"This where you usually eat?" Clint asked. "Pull up a chair, unless you're afraid of us, like everyone else."

Riggs pulled out a chair and sat down. The waiter immediately appeared with a steak dinner.

"Looks like they were expecting you," Clint said.

"I always eat here the same time every day," Riggs said, "only it ain't usually this empty."

"Our fault, I guess," Clint said.

"I'll tip big," Reeves said, "to try to make up for it."

"Well, the word is around town," Riggs said. "Nobody's on the street. They're all inside, waiting to see who's gonna make the first move, you or the Buffalo Soldiers."

"They ain't Buffalo Soldiers no more," Reeves said with feeling.

"Well," Riggs said, "sorry, but that's how people around here think of them."

"Yeah, well . . ."

"Don't mind him," Clint said. "He's been after these men a long time."

"If you don't mind me askin'," Riggs said, "when will you be facin' them?" Then he added, "I'm askin' on behalf of the town."

"Soon," Reeves said.

"We're waiting to see if they'll blink first," Clint explained. Riggs didn't look like he understood. "We just want to make them a little nervous."

"Ah," Riggs said, "well, the whole town is nervous, that's for sure."

"We're sorry about that," Reeves said. "We'll do our best to get this over with as fast as we can so the people in town can feel safe again."

They finished their pie and coffee while Riggs was still eating his steak.

"We'll leave you to your meal," Clint said as he and Reeves stood up.

"I'll be listenin' for shots," Riggs said. "Lots of them."

"You'll hear them," Clint said, "unless all six of those men just surrender."

Riggs laughed. "What's the chance of that?" he asked.

"Yeah, you're right," Clint said. "What are the chances?"

He and Reeves left the café.

Outside the street was still deserted. They stopped just in front of the café door.

"I have a suggestion," Clint said.

"What's that?" Reeves asked.

"Let me call the play."

"Why?"

"Because," Clint said, "you and Washington know each other."

"Yeah."

"Have you heard of the game called chess?"

"No," Reeves said, "just poker."

"Well, this isn't with cards, it's on a board . . . actually, I really don't know how to play it myself, but I know that it's about strategy. You and Washington can figure out each other's strategies."

"Okay, I think I see what you mean," Reeves said. "If you call the play, he won't be able to predict it."

"Exactly."

Reeves thought a moment, then said, "Well, yeah, okay. Let's do that, 'cause right now Washington and me have got us all sittin' around doin' nothin'."

"That's why," Clint said, "I think we should do *something*."

"But what?"

"Come on," Clint said. "I'll tell you my plan on the way."

FORTY-ONE

Clint took a deep breath and walked through the batwing doors. Inside six black men and one white man turned their eyes toward him.

"Can I get a beer in here?" he asked.

"Sure," Washington said. "Make room at the bar for Mr. Adams, boys."

There was plenty of room so they didn't really have to move. The bartender—the only other white man in the place—set a beer on the bar for Clint and implored him with his eyes to give him some help.

Clint picked up the beer left-handed, turned, and looked at Washington and Jefferson.

"Where's your buddy?" Washington asked. "Where's Bass Reeves?"

Clint sipped his beer, said, "To tell you the truth, I don't know where he is right now."

"Is that a fact?" Washington asked. "Gordon, check the back door of this place."

"Yessir."

"Take somebody with you."

Gordon looked at Weatherby, who nodded. The two men headed for the back of the saloon.

"You think I'm lying?" Clint asked.

"The next thing you'll tell me is that you and Bass had a fight," Washington said, "and you ain't backin' his play no more."

"Why would I tell you that?" Clint asked. "Bass is my friend. Of course I'm backing his play."

"Then what are you doin' here?"

"Maybe this is his play."

"And he's comin' in the back while you keep us busy? That ain't much of a plan."

"I agree," Clint said. "That wouldn't be much of a plan."

Gordon and Weatherby returned.

"Ain't nothin' happenin' back there, Sarge," he said. "The rear door is locked up tight, and ain't no broken windows."

"All right," Washington said. "Check upstairs. See if Reeves came in through a window up there."

Both Gordon and Weatherby looked up at the ceiling, then back at Washington.

"All right," he said, "all four of you go!"

The four black men moved away from the bar and went up the stairs to the second floor.

"Check every room!" Washington shouted.

"We will," Gordon said.

In a few moments they could hear the footsteps above them as the men went from room to room.

In the saloon there were now only two black men, Jefferson and Washington. Clint stood at the bar, a half-finished beer in his left hand. He was watching the two seated men. The bartender stood behind the bar, watching all three of them.

Washington and Jefferson watched Clint, then seemed to realize that they had gone from a six-to-one advantage to two-to-one.

Which against the Gunsmith was a disadvantage.

"Wait a minute," Jefferson said. He started to get up and go for his gun.

"Corporal—" Washington said warningly.

Jefferson didn't listen. He pushed his chair back and put his hand on his gun.

That was when the batwing doors swung open and Bass Reeves entered the saloon.

FORTY-TWO

Washington suddenly realized what the plan had been, to divide him and his men by making him think Clint was there to distract them.

"Easy," he said to Jefferson, who had not quite drawn his gun.

Reeves looked at Washington.

"This wasn't your plan," Washington said.

"No," Reeves said, "it was Clint's. Jefferson, take your hand away from your gun."

Jefferson was frozen in place, his hand on his gun.

Washington was chuckling and shaking his head.

"You let him call the play," he said. "I didn't expect that."

Clint could hear the footsteps above them.

"They're coming back," Clint said. "You two drop your guns now."

Washington was staring at Reeves. Jefferson was watching Clint.

"Put your guns down now!" Reeves said.

Washington knew they needed only minutes for the others to come down.

"Jefferson . . ." he said.

Washington leaped to his feet as Jefferson went for his gun.

Clint and Bass Reeves drew.

Washington grabbed Jefferson from behind and used him as a shield. The corporal realized what was happening too late. As Washington dragged him back toward the rear of the saloon, Clint and Reeves fired. Washington felt the slugs strike Jefferson's body. The corporal squeezed off a couple of shots into the ground.

When Washington reached the door in the back wall of the saloon, he shoved the dead corporal away from him.

At that moment the other four soldiers, hearing the shots, came running down the stairs, their guns in their hands. When they saw Clint and Reeves, they started firing.

Clint threw himself over the bar, landed on the bartender.

"Stay down," he told the man.

"Don't worry, I will."

Reeves had backed out of the saloon, took cover outside so he could fire over the batwing doors.

The four men scattered, overturned tables to use as cover. But they were cheap tables. Clint rose up and fired three shots into one of them. The bullets went right through and killed Weatherby.

Reeves, seeing what happened, picked out an overturned table and fired four shots into it. They went through and killed Gordon.

"Give it up!" he shouted. "Those tables give you no cover."

He and Clint waited a few moments, then fired high into the tables to illustrate their point.

"Okay, okay," Webster shouted. "Stop firing."

"Toss out your guns."

Webster threw his over the table. They waited, and then Franklin did the same thing.

Reeves stepped into the saloon. Clint stood up.

"I've got them," he said. "Go after Washington."

"Thanks," Reeves said.

He ran out of the saloon.

Washington heard all the shooting in the saloon as he went out the back door. He could have run around to the front of the saloon and tried to get behind Reeves and Clint Adams. Instead, he ran straight for the livery stable.

Reeves came out of the saloon watching for Washington to appear. He would have gone out the back and then run around to the front. That's what he would have done, and what most Buffalo Soldiers would have done.

Washington would do the opposite.

Washington reached the livery on the run. The stable was empty, so he found his horse's stall and started saddling it.

"It's not gonna be that easy, Lem," Reeves said.

Washington froze, then turned, saw Reeves standing in the doorway.

"You can't outthink me," Reeves said. "You wanna see if you can outdraw me?"

"Adams'll be here any minute," Washington said.

"He's takin' care of the rest of your men," Reeves said. "What did you promise them to get them to follow you? Money? A big score?"

"I got them money," Washington said. "The bank here was supposed to be a big score."

"Now you'll never know."

"I will if I kill you, and then Adams."

"That's a tall order, even for a Buffalo Soldier."

Washington turned away from his horse to face Reeves.

"Well," he said, "I might as well get by you first."

"I don't understand you, Lem," Reeves said. "You were a Buffalo Soldier."

"We were still puppets, Bass," Washington said, "with white men pullin' the strings. Hell, your strings are bein' pulled by Judge Parker. Another white man."

"I got no strings."

"You think you don't—"

"You won't convince me," Reeves said. "Not like you did the rest of your men. Four of them are dead, and you used one of them as a shield."

"It was his duty to help his CO escape."

"What you did was the act of a coward, Lem," Reeves said. "Now drop your gun. I'm takin' you back."

"To hang? Not likely. I ain't lettin' no white man hang me."

"Then it ends here."

Washington nodded.

"We agree on that, Bass. It ends here."

Clint turned the remaining two men over to Sheriff Riggs and ran out of the saloon. The only place he could think Washington would go was the livery.

As he approached the stable on the run, he heard a shot. He increased his speed, but stopped short of the door. He drew his gun and moved slowly, peering into the stable. He saw one black man standing over another.

Reeves turned his head and looked at him.

"It's over," he said. "He wouldn't go back."

Clint walked in, holstering his gun. He looked down at the dead Lem Washington.

"Well," he said to the black deputy, "at least you have two live ones to bring back to the Judge. He can still have himself a hanging party."

"You think the Judge enjoys hangin' men?"

"I think he does, yeah," Clint said. "Why else is he always insisting you bring them back alive?"

Reeves studied Clint for a few moments, then said, "That's somethin' we'll have to talk about another time. I have ta get those last two back to Fort Smith."

"I'm not coming," Clint said. "I've already spend too much time in the Territories."

"Where are you gonna go?"

"I don't know," Clint said. "Maybe I'll head back to Texas."

Reeves stuck his hand out.

"Thanks for everythin' you did."

Clint shook his hand.

"Give my best to the Judge," he said.

Watch for

THE DEATH LIST

363rd novel in the exciting GUNSMITH series
from Jove

Coming in March!

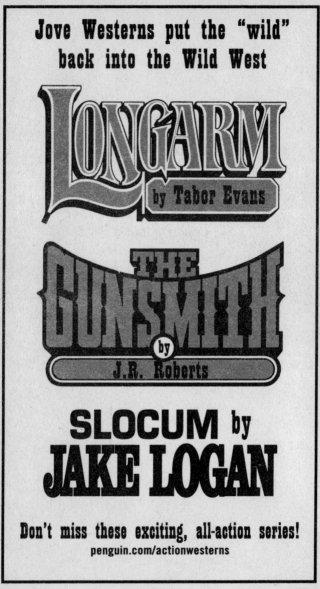